Dylan growled, "Of course she's taking the ranch."

Then he pulled her out of the office and stuffed her in his truck. After he slammed his own door, he let out a long, gusty breath and started the engine.

"I don't believe it."

His jaw clenched. "Neither do I."

"He didn't really. . ."

"He did. You got it." Dylan kept staring ahead. "What's your address?"

She stammered her cross streets. "You know I didn't—" She shook her head. "I don't understand. I didn't know."

Finally, he shot her a sideways glance. The muscle in his cheek twitched, and his lips pressed together. Determination, grudging as it sounded, finally echoed in his curt words. "What's done is done. I'll pull you through for a year."

Sondra swallowed hard. She'd been a charity case all of her life and struggled so hard to be self-sufficient. The depth of his upset was clear, even if he'd not voiced a word of it. "You expected more."

CATHY MARIE HAKE is a Southern California native who loves her work as a nurse and Lamaze teacher. She and her husband have a daughter, a son, and three dogs, so life is never dull or quiet. Cathy considers herself a sentimental packrat, collecting antiques and Hummel figurines. In spare moments, she reads, bargain hunts, and makes a huge mess with her new hobby of scrapbooking. Cathy@CathyMarieHake.com

Books by Cathy Marie Hake

In His Will

Cathy Marie Hake

Heartsong Presents

A note from the Author:
I love to hear from my readers! You may correspond with me by writing:

Cathy Marie Hake
Author Relations
PO Box 721
Uhrichsville, OH 44683

ISBN 1-59310-898-2

IN HIS WILL

Our mission is to publish and distribute inspirational products offering exceptional value and biblical encouragement to the masses.

PRINTED IN THE U.S.A.

one

"The old man's gone to the Big Daddy in the sky."

Dylan Ward winced. The opening remark set the tone for a memorial service that turned into a full-fledged travesty. No respect. No reverence. No words of redemption. Their pastor from back home got sick, so the funeral home hastily plugged in a replacement. Though he didn't hold with judging another man's walk with the Lord, Dylan suspected this so-called preacher had gotten his degree from a matchbook cover. While leading them in the Lord's Prayer, he flubbed the recitation in several spots.

Following that debacle, Miller Quintain's relatives each gave eulogies revolving around memories of his financial generosity. Their words became a can-you-top-this, he-loved-me-most competition.

Unwilling to let a good friend's life be summed up in such shallow terms, Dylan rose and buttoned his suit coat as he walked to the front of the chapel. Turning to face the small collection of people, he caught sight of a woman who must have slipped in late. She sat at the very back, alone. Over her black dress, she wore a blue-and-green plaid flannel shirt. Everything about this funeral was surreal.

Dylan looked at the rose-decked casket, then faced the room. "When I was seven, Miller Quintain told me a man can live with gritty hands and muddy boots, but he's got to have a clean heart. . . ."

A short while later, Miller's relatives jockeyed for one of the four seats at the graveside. If last night's storm hadn't softened the hard-packed Oklahoma soil, their crocodile tears could. Dylan stood off to the side and understood why Miller specified the service was for family only. He'd been a simple man who didn't want a lot of fuss and wouldn't want the folks back home to witness a circus like this.

Things would get much worse before the day ended. After several years of open discussion, Dylan knew what Quintain's will would hold. Miller warned him to expect a nasty scene once these greedy relatives discovered they weren't inheriting his fortune.

The woman in the flannel shirt walked the long way around the cemetery and silently took a place a few feet from Dylan. High cheekbones and slightly slanted green eyes set her apart—she didn't look anything like Miller's relatives. She'd put her mahogany-red-colored hair into a sophisticated bun at the top of her head and probably used half a can of hairspray today to keep it under control. Small wisps teased their way free and coiled into twirly, springy tendrils.

The way she clutched a bunch of wildflowers to her heart touched Dylan—not only because of her sorrow, but also because of the devotion it revealed. Instead of buying something, she must've gotten up early to gather the bouquet from the Oklahoma countryside Miller had loved. Silently, she slipped forward, laid the offering by the head of the casket, and stepped back.

The substitute showed up and nervously rubbed his hands together. "You've already said your good-byes. It's an emotional time. Why don't we say the Twenty-second Psalm together in closing?" He looked at the redhead. "Do you know it? Would you like to start us off?"

She gave him a baffled look, seemed to think for a moment, and slowly nodded. "My God, my God, why have you forsaken me? Why are you so far from saving me, so far from the words of my groaning? O my God, I cry out by day, but you do not answer, by night, and am not silent."

"No, no. That's not it." The preacher's brows beetled.

Dylan looked at the woman, astonished she'd been able

to remember that passage. "What about the Twenty-third Psalm?" They made eye contact, and she nodded. He started out, and she joined in, "The Lord is my shepherd. . ."

At least they could make this right.

&

Sondra Thankful huddled in Kenny's old shirt. It offered little solace. Grief crashed over her. First her husband, then her dear friend, Miller. *God, why is it Your will for me to be alone?*

The minute the prayer ended, Miller's relatives started to bicker. Sondra backed away from the ugliness. She'd forgotten how her heels sank into the ground at Kenny's funeral until they did the same thing now.

"Careful." The tall man who'd recited the Psalm braced her elbow for a moment. From what he said during the service, she knew who he was: Dylan, the neighbor Miller thought of as a son.

Sondra subtly took stock of him. His warmth and spicy aftershave filled her senses as his six-foot height and broad frame blocked the wind. Steady gray eyes seemed to search out details and file them away, and the shadow on his square jaw made it look as though he'd spent a less than restful night. The wind played havoc with his fine black hair, and his charcoal gray suit jacket gaped as he raised a hand to shove back a lock of it. He looked ill-at-ease in the suit, and freshly polished cowboy boots made it clear where he'd rather be.

"I'm Dylan Ward. Miller was my neighbor."

"I'm Sondra Thankful. Miller spoke very highly of you, Dylan."

"That means a lot—especially today." He studied her for a long moment. "He was pretty cryptic about you. All I know is that you're a teacher and volunteer at a children's group home here in Lawton. He used to loan you baby chicks."

"Mmm-hmm. I posted a note in several feed stores, asking if someone would let me borrow chicks for troubled children to hold. Only one rancher in the whole area responded—Miller Quintain."

"That's Miller," Dylan confirmed with a decisive nod. "The man had a knack for filling the empty places in other people's lives."

"He did." She turned to stare at the horizon.

"Why chicks?"

"They're teeny and light—quiet, too. Even the smallest child can cradle one. It's great therapy for kids who've gotten beaten up by life. When they feel completely out of control, it helps to have something soft and warm to hold on to."

Dylan's gaze dropped to her hand. Sondra hadn't realized she'd bunched the flannel shirttail in her palm until his eyes narrowed. Just as quickly, compassion softened his features.

"Excuse me." Overwhelmed by grief, Sondra barely choked out the words and turned away. Her heel sank in the grass as she buried her face in her hands and wept.

"Whoa. Easy there." Dylan gathered her closer to his side and cradled her head to his chest. He didn't shush her or even say anything more; he merely held her as she sobbed. When she started to calm down, he pressed a handkerchief into her hands. "Here."

"Thanks." She pulled away and dabbed at her eyes. "I'm going to miss him so much."

"So will I." Dylan's solemn voice carried the ache of deep loss. Sondra sensed his presence at her side as they walked across the cemetery.

A man in a custom-tailored suit who'd been on the fringes of the funeral stood at the curb. He raised his voice because of the wind. "Are you Sondra Thankful?"

"Yes."

"I'm Geoffrey Cheviot of Cheviot, Masters, and Associates. My apologies that I relied on my secretary to call you. You are coming back to the office?"

Sondra gave him a baffled look. "I don't belong."

"Mr. Quintain was an old-fashioned man. He specified his last will and testament was to be read following the service." The attorney's face reflected no emotion as he added, "Miller requested you be present."

"Who is she, anyway?" one woman wondered aloud. Miller Quintain's relatives all suddenly focused on her—but their interest carried more malevolence than curiosity.

Dylan gently curled his hand around Sondra's elbow. He kept his voice low. "Come—for Miller."

Put in that light, she didn't give it further consideration. "I'll be there."

The attorney smiled with unmistakable relief. "Good. I'll see you at the office."

Dylan kept hold of Sondra and headed toward the parking lot. She inched closer to him, both for warmth and protection. The wind carried a chill, but the stares of Miller's relatives were downright frigid. Dylan halted for a split second to allow the wind to buffet a crinkling sheet of newspaper across their path, then continued on. "Which car is yours?"

"My ride's just around the corner."

He leaned forward and looked past her. "The bus?" Incredulity filled his voice.

"My car's in the shop."

"I'll give you a ride." He nodded decisively. "We'll swap stories about Miller." He strode along until they made it to a well-kept, older pickup.

"I can take the bus. Really."

Dylan shook his head. "I'll put you in a cab. You can't wait in the cold and ride on a crowded bus."

She couldn't afford to pay for a cab. *Miller trusted him, and the lawyer knows I'm with him.* She gave him a sad smile. "I'm not very good company today."

"Neither am I. Here." He unlocked and opened the door.

Once in the truck, Sondra fell silent. They both stared out of the windshield. Yesterday's thunderstorm hadn't lost steam until early this morning, and the clouds hung low, like ominous, gray monoliths in the vast Oklahoma sky. Dreariness coated Lawton as Dylan drove through the streets.

He turned on the radio. A quartet sang "Rock of Ages" *a cappella.* "This okay with you?"

"Yes. Comforting, even."

Sondra's thoughts wandered aimlessly, and Dylan seemed equally content with the silence. The hymn ended and another began. *I should ask him to tell me more about Miller. Hearing about Miller would—*

"How long did you know Miller?"

"Just about two years." She smiled at the memory. "The first time we met, I thought he looked like the man on the Luden's cough drop box."

Dylan chuckled. They spent the next fifteen minutes remembering their friend. Dylan pulled to the curb and announced, "Here we are."

"Thanks for the ride. Sharing memories like that has helped me."

"Me, too."

She shrugged. "I don't see why I'm here."

"Miller was a generous man. He may have left you a bit of money so you could keep taking the baby chicks to the kids."

"It'd be great. They really make a difference."

He nodded. "Yeah, I'll bet they do. Tell you what—I don't have a coop, but if Miller didn't arrange for you to keep getting chicks, I'll put one in, and you're welcome to come pick them up just like you did before."

Her lips parted in surprise. "Wow. Thanks!" As he shut his door, she took a couple of deep breaths, then whispered, "Lord, I could really use Your help here. You know—courage and strength. . ." As soon as she unlocked her door, Dylan helped her out.

Geoffrey Cheviot personally met them at the door for the building. "If you'll follow me. . ." He led them to the law offices and into a sizable corner meeting room. Plush, camel-colored carpeting muffled their steps, and the oppressive gray from the sky filtered through the wall-to-wall plate glass windows. Several chairs sat in a semicircle facing an oak wall unit. Gesturing toward a pair of chairs closest to the door, he invited, "Please be seated."

Sondra lowered herself into one of them and tucked her purse on the floor. Mr. Cheviot returned with the family members, and she shifted in her seat. *I don't belong here with the friends and family.*

The staid-looking attorney waited until everyone settled into the seats, then opened the center doors of the wall unit to reveal a large television screen. He pulled a CD from a nearby shelf. "Miller Quintain has a written testament. You will all receive copies, but he also recorded it. He wanted to express his wishes to you directly. I'll play it for you now."

The sight of Miller's sunbaked, laugh-wrinkled face made Sondra suck in a quick breath. Dylan must have heard that soft gasp, because he slid his big, rough hand over and gently patted her arm.

Miller stared into the camera and spoke as he always had—straight, to the point, and with a minimum of fuss. "Well, folks, this is it. My will is absolutely airtight. Settle for what I give you, or challenge my wishes and receive a single dollar for your gall. That being said, let me make it clear I just came from the doctor, and he's certified me as being completely of sound mind. This is what I want done with all that I've amassed."

"The old coot never did have any class," one relative muttered.

Miller rattled off the names of seven relatives, then drawled, "You never much bothered with me while I was alive, so I'm not feeling it necessary to fret much over your welfare, either. Getting here for the funeral set you back a tad, so I'm leaving each of you three thousand dollars to cover expenses. Consider yourselves lucky to get that much out of me. It's a better return on those annual Christmas cards than you deserve."

The room erupted. Angry shouts, cries, and growls filled the air. "Silence, please!" Mr. Cheviot demanded.

Miller continued on, "Edwin, as my brother, you never did have it in you to completely forget me. I know my money interested you far more than my companionship, but I want you to have one last go at something, so I'm bequeathing you fifty grand."

"Fifty grand! Is that all?"

The image on the monitor spoke on. "Then I come to Dylan Ward. Dylan. . ." Miller paused. A kind smile creased his weather-beaten face, making him look just the way Sondra remembered him. It was eerie to see the fondness and compassionate quality looming there when they'd just buried him. His lips moved, "Dylan, I think of you as being the son I never had."

Dylan's hand slid away from her arm. For some inexplicable reason, she had an almost overwhelming urge to snatch it back.

"The antique gun collection is yours. My horse and saddle—you've admired them, and I want them to go to you. Oh—and the gray enamel coffeepot? You know where to find it. It's yours, Dylan.

"I hope you'll understand." Miller chuckled roughly. "Come to think of it, you probably won't understand for a while, but I trust you will someday. I'm not going along with my original plan.

"I'm leaving you the easternmost two hundred acres and thirty percent of the value of my livestock, all to be granted to you one year from today—under one condition: the Curly Q must achieve the same annual profit margin for this fiscal year as it has averaged in the past five. Mr. Cheviot has the parameters in a file for your reference."

Sondra couldn't tear her gaze from Miller's image. She heard the rough sound of Dylan clearing his throat. She didn't care what Miller and he had worked out. It wasn't any of her business. Miller had a right to do what he wanted, but she sensed something about this arrangement came as a huge blow.

"That brings me to Sondra Thankful."

two

Everyone in the room turned and stared at her. Dylan was no exception.

"Sondra, sugar, you made these last years the happiest ones of my life. We were kindred spirits who weathered life's storms on our own terms. My only regret is that I'm not there to give you some help, but I'm trusting Dylan to fill in for me." He chuckled again in that odd, rasping way he'd had. "He'll be forced to since I've saddled him with leaving the livestock on my land during the next year. You can rely on him. He has a sound head on his shoulders."

Sondra felt the blood seep from her face in slow degrees as Miller's voice droned on. "As for the balance of my estate, real and personal—home, ranch, and possessions as well as the remaining livestock and balance of funds—I leave them all in total to Sondra Thankful with two provisions: She is to take immediate possession and live at the Curly Q for the next full year, and the ranch must reach the profit level I mentioned earlier. If those conditions aren't met, Mr. Cheviot will give Sondra fifteen thousand dollars, then accept the offer from Tuttlesworth Developers to turn the land into a housing subdivision."

A ruckus ensued. Dylan shot to his feet, scooped her purse from the floor, and shoved it in her numb hands. "Let's go."

"But—"

Dylan took hold of her arm, yanked her from the room, and steered her through the office. Mr. Cheviot scurried alongside them, blurting out two alternatives they'd not heard because of the ruckus. He'd just finished telling them Sondra could immediately opt out for fifteen grand or, "You and Mr.

Ward can marry and have full, unconditional possession." He looked at Sondra expectantly.

Dylan growled, "Of course she's taking the ranch." Then he pulled her out of the office and stuffed her in his truck. After he slammed his own door, he let out a long, gusty breath and started the engine.

"I don't believe it."

His jaw clenched. "Neither do I."

"He didn't really. . ."

"He did. You got it." Dylan kept staring ahead. "What's your address?"

She stammered her cross streets. "You know I didn't—" She shook her head. "I don't understand. I didn't know."

Finally, he shot her a sideways glance. The muscle in his cheek twitched, and his lips pressed together. Determination, grudging as it sounded, finally echoed in his curt words. "What's done is done. I'll pull you through for a year."

Sondra swallowed hard. She'd been a charity case all of her life and struggled so hard to be self-sufficient. The depth of his upset was clear, even if he'd not voiced a word of it. "You expected more."

His long fingers tightened around the steering wheel. "No. Absolutely not. And yes. We didn't have it on paper. There was an understanding. I've already made arrangements for a loan; I planned to buy all of the Curly Q, and the money was to fund Miller's favorite charities."

"I see."

"No, you don't." He hit the turn signal indicator with notable force. The clicking sounded preternaturally loud until he made a right turn and it automatically shut off. Though clearly upset, he kept his voice so carefully modulated and low, it gave her the willies. "I need the land."

Shocked by the whole turn of events, Sondra stared out the windshield. Month by month, she barely eked by. In one incredibly generous gesture, Miller rescued her. *A home.*

I'll have a home. None of it seemed real. She cast a glance at Dylan. The set of his jaw and way his fingers curled in a near death grip around the steering wheel made it clear her windfall was his loss. "I'm sorry the will ruined your plans."

He slowly eased his hold and flexed long, callused fingers. "Not ruined. Delayed." He nodded resolutely, as if confirming something to himself, and kept his eyes trained on the road. "As soon as we're through this year, that acreage will be mine; but I may as well put my offer on the table here and now—I want first bidding rights to buy the rest off of you when we finish the contract year."

Her chin lifted. He'd stung her with that demand. By willing her that land, Miller gave her a home—the one thing she'd never had. "I'm not going to sell it."

"Don't get your dander up. The original agreement I reached with Miller stipulated the money would go to a charity. This way, you'll get it instead."

"So instead of *worthy* causes, *I've* turned out to be Miller's 'charity.'"

"It's none of my business. As I said, what's done is done. Like it or not, we're partners for the next year." A wry smile twisted his lips. "Actually, it's a little shy of a year. The Curly Q is set up so the fiscal year hits in mid-March. I reckon we can tolerate each other that long."

"Not necessarily. I can turn down the ranch and take the fifteen thousand dollars Mr. Cheviot mentioned."

He snorted. "That's as likely as us getting married."

"No kidding," she snapped.

"Okay, I'm sorry. I can't believe Miller even put that as an option. I've got more pride and sense than to marry a woman to get land. Judging from today, you're still reeling from your own loss."

"Maybe I should just hire a consultant."

Dylan pulled his truck to an abrupt stop next to her apartment building. He twisted to face her, his eyes alight with ire.

"Not a chance, lady. You stick some idiot in there who messes things up, and the profit margin will be too low. You're not putting my future in someone else's hands."

"So you expect me to place my future in your hands?"

"You got that straight." He slid out of the truck and opened her door. Towering over her, he gritted, "Get it in your pretty little head right now: I'm running the show."

"Not unless I say so. I could take the money and let the developers cement in the whole place!" Sondra marched to her apartment, let herself in, and shut the door. A glance showed Dylan standing on the pavement, his hands on his hips and a scowl darkening his much-too-handsome features. If she accepted the conditions of the will and kept control of her life and affairs, she'd have an enemy for a neighbor.

Two hours later, Sondra looked around her cramped apartment. Her teacher's salary qualified as modest, and hefty college loans ate into her budget. Fifteen thousand dollars would barely get her out of debt. Financially, she needed to work—and she'd be forced to leave the baby with a sitter all of the time once it came. *On the ranch, I can be a full-time mother. Miller did that for you and me, sweetie.*

She slumped on the sofa and rested her hand over her slightly rounded tummy. Just last week, she'd started to wear maternity clothes. They weren't absolutely necessary, but some of her regular clothes felt binding. Three months of morning sickness had made her weight dip dangerously. Then, too, grieving didn't do much for her appetite. Most women looked noticeably pregnant by the beginning of their sixth month.

Lord, I don't know what to do. Guide me.

In the quiet, reality started to sink in. *Miller's friendship was such a blessing. When everything else fell apart, he cared and showed God's love to me. I've been praying for months now. I've asked God to show me His will. Could this be it?*

By taking the ranch, she'd have to work hard—but that was nothing new. With this, she'd be financially stable. She'd have a place all of her own, a forever-ours home in which to rear her son, and they wouldn't have to scrimp from week to week. Of all the people Miller knew, all the lives he touched, he'd singled her out. Why? She'd never know, but she'd eternally be grateful.

What did she know about ranching? She was twenty-five and never once rode a horse. Cattle were cute, splotchy animals in picture books. Yes, she did a creditable *moo* sound. Other than that, ignorance abounded.

The simple fact of the matter hit hard—she needed to enlist some sound help. Miller planned on having her go to Dylan Ward for advice. She ought to abide by Miller's wishes—even though Dylan had gotten overbearing. Truth was, she needed him.

Regardless of his dissatisfaction with the will, Dylan needed to work with her. He had too much riding on it—thirty percent of the value of the livestock and an awesome chunk of land, to be precise. If he tried to take his anger out on her, he'd be cheating himself, too. Whether she liked Dylan or not, Miller trusted him. That was the best endorsement she could get. For whatever reason, Miller bound them together in the deal, and their futures hinged on cooperating to keep the Curly Q profitable. Her child's future depended on things working out, so she was going to have to set aside her ironclad rule of self-determination and control.

She splayed her fingers over her tummy and slowly rubbed a few circles. "Miller did this so I could be there for you all of the time. Maybe that's God's plan, too. For you, my little one, I'll do anything."

She took the business card the lawyer discreetly slipped into her pocket, picked up the telephone, and dialed. "Mr. Cheviot? This is Sondra Thankful. I've decided to move to the Curly Q as soon as we take care of the arrangements."

❧

Dylan dumped a bale of hay onto the barn floor. The wire snapped, just like his temper. How could Miller do this to him? He'd arranged long ago for the loan it would take to gain the greater portion of the land. He owned sufficient collateral and kept enough in the bank to swing the deal. No one knew the land better; no one loved it more. He didn't *want* a handout. Hadn't expected one. Accustomed to working hard for everything he ever got, Dylan never once presumed that Miller would simply hand over the ranch. Still, he'd said things over the years which made it clear that he fully expected Dylan to own the land when he was gone.

The strange bequest came as such a shock. A nasty one, at that. Even worse, it went to a city-girl. She'd foul things up so badly, the Curly Q wouldn't be worth a plug nickel in a year. It would serve her right for him to let her flounder.

Then Dylan looked out of the open barn door. Land was too precious to be squandered, too dear to be misused. Livestock was certainly too valuable to be mistreated. . .and thirty percent of the value of that livestock waited for him at the end of the year. He couldn't let all of that go to rack and ruin any more than he could chop off his right arm. Kicking the hay, he bitterly accepted Miller had counted on that very fact.

Even worse, the thought of the land being leveled, cemented, and turned into row upon row of cookie-cutter tract homes made his blood curdle. He loved standing in a field and seeing nothing but God's beautiful earth for almost as far as the eye could see. Marring this with noise, traffic, and houses—*never*. Sondra actually threatened yesterday that she could opt for the fifteen grand and let the land go to the developers. Whatever it took, Dylan vowed he'd make certain the land wasn't violated like that.

What it would take was honoring Miller's request. He'd call and reason with her. For the sake of a dead friend's last request, Dylan would do it.

"Okay. I bail her out for one stinking year," he muttered under his breath. "I'm not letting her hire someone to run the show, though. That's asking far too much."

ʚ•

Sondra carried in her suitcase, set it on the bed, and opened the window. Sunshine filtered through the dusty window and a breeze made the brown paisley curtains sway. She looked around with a sense of awe.

She'd been in the house on several occasions, but most of the rooms were closed off. Taking a tentative tour, she decided to occupy the master bedroom and turn the adjacent bedroom into a nursery. The third bedroom looked to be a guest room, so it could be left alone. Miller had converted the fourth bedroom into an office, and she felt a spurt of relief at the neatly arranged books and files that would help guide her through the next year. The kitchen looked old, but serviceable. The gouges in the walnut coffee table reminded her of Miller's habit of propping his feet up. The house felt lived-in and comfortable. *God, You've blessed me far beyond what I ever dreamed of.*

She traipsed down the stairs into the basement and noted with glee that the washer and dryer were in good condition. The far corner boasted an iron-reinforced, cement tornado shelter. Once, last spring, when the skies turned an ugly green and hail started falling, Miller had grabbed her and taken her there for safety. Yes, safety. This house was a monument to the security God was providing for her and the baby. Sondra came back upstairs, made a few quick phone calls, then went out into the yard.

Unsure where to start, Sondra headed for the henhouse. She'd been there dozens of times, and it shouldn't be too hard to gather eggs. The hens seemed crazy, squawking and trying to get out of the door. Fifteen minutes later, her wrists pecked raw, Sondra reached into the last nest. She jerked back with a shriek as a snake slithered from the bits of hay.

Nothing, but nothing, could keep her there. Sondra rocketed out of the door, screaming bloody murder. She careened straight into none other than Dylan Ward.

three

"Snake!"

He braced her slender arms for a moment, then drawled, "Are you calling me names, or is there a snake in the henhouse?"

Wide-eyed, she stood there.

Grit beneath his boots scraped loudly as Dylan set Sondra aside. He strode into the henhouse and came back out holding a squirming, twenty-inch reptile. Extending it toward her, he grinned. "This is a common milk snake. They've been known to eat eggs. They certainly don't eat people. If anything, the poor thing is terrified of you. You sure can kick up a powerful fuss."

Sondra made a strangled sound.

"Any time you see a snake, just walk the other way or grab a hoe and chop off his head. Here by the stable, be sure to kill 'em, because they spook the horses." Taking his own advice, Dylan tossed down the snake, armed himself with a hoe, and beheaded it. He then picked up the body and hung it over the nearest fence rail where it continued to squirm.

Sondra barely made it around to the back of the barn before she lost her breakfast.

Dylan shoved a bandanna at her so she could wipe her face. "I suppose I ought to be glad you got that out of your system straight off. The rest of the day probably won't go any better."

"What are you doing here?"

"I came to show you around. I've already checked on the horses, and Joseph's mucking out the stable. You have plenty to do. Someone needs to clean out the water troughs. They're getting slimy."

Sondra closed her eyes and swayed a bit.

He felt a little sorry when she turned green after his last comment. After all, she'd just thrown up. Then again, he wasn't about to handle matters for her just because she felt queasy.

As if she dreaded asking, she gulped before asking, "What else?"

"Chickens—they aren't a profitable venture. Most ranches that run beeves don't mess with poultry, but Miller was soft-hearted. He did it and donated the eggs to the Texas food bank. A local man picks them up as a public service. It's a fair bit of work with no financial return. You could get a piddly sum if you sold off those hens and the incubator in the hatchery, but the coop and stuff would have to be trashed."

Without hesitation, she said, "I'm not selling. I want to continue with Miller's plan. We loved what we were doing with those chicks."

"Caring for them takes time."

She looked him in the eye. "I make time for what's important to me."

"Even if the chickens are a pittance, it's going to cost you money. You'll have to hire someone in to keep them for you. I've temporarily assigned my man, Luna, to cover for you since he grew up on a spread that kept laying hens."

"Thanks. I'll start learning right away so I can assume full responsibility. I expect to pay his wages in the meantime."

At least she's not shutting down a charity operation or asking for any more favors.

Sondra gave one of the yard dogs a pat on the head. He was an ugly mongrel with a naturally mean-looking sneer, but she didn't seem in the least bit afraid. Chickens and dogs—at least she wasn't afraid of every small creature—just snakes.

"I called the library, and they're setting aside books on cows for me."

He tried to quell the smile, but it wasn't possible. "You're going to read up on everything?"

"Yes, I am."

"Fine. Until you cuddle up with those books, schoolteacher, let me give you a glimpse at the real thing." He took her around the ranch. They didn't go far; she needed to get a feel for the major setup before he bogged her down with details, however important they might be.

"Instead of taking Pretty Boy to my stable, I'll leave him here. Times when I drive over and need a mount, he'll be available."

Sondra nodded. "When can you take the guns?"

"I brought my truck today."

"I'll leave the house unlocked. Were there other things you'd like—anything with sentimental value?"

He hooked his thumbs in his belt loops. "I got the coffee-pot. I'm happy."

Patting another dog, she said, "Holler if you think of anything else." She straightened. "Back to business—when's payday for the hands?"

Dylan gave her an assessing look. "Know much about computers?"

"Enough to get by."

"Miller kept spread sheets, feed records, supply lists, and the like computerized. I'll keep you informed so you can update them." He locked eyes with her to underscore the significance of what he said next. "Most important thing you'll do is payroll. Payday is every other Friday; you'll need to cut the men checks this week. Miller paid his men well, and they earn every cent of it."

She nodded. Funny how she wasn't overly talkative like most women he knew. Kind of kept to herself.

Dylan continued his instructions. "Most ranches end up with a fair percentage of drifters, but your crew is long-term and steady. Keep it that way. They'll manage nicely with supervision." *Mine*, he silently vowed. The minute he'd learned Sondra took up residence, Dylan had hightailed on over to reinforce his position. Resolved to fulfill Miller's directive, he wasn't about to let this city-gal plug someone else into a position of authority. Judging from how her men nodded or greeted him, they'd already accepted his presence.

"Dylan?"

"Yeah?"

She stared up at him somberly. "I don't like being dependent. I know it's not much, but I'd be happy to take on your spread's bookkeeping and payroll duties, too."

She took him by surprise with her offer, but he didn't want her dabbling in his business. "My sister, Teresa, handles all of that for me."

"Oh. I'd like to meet her."

"She's staying with a friend for a few days, shopping and stuff. I'm sure she'll come by when she gets back."

Dylan squinted at the horizon and watched a calf wobble around on unsteady legs. Kinda like this woman—so brand-spankin' new to the world, she didn't even have solid footing.

"Out here, we're tight-knit. The Merriweathers have the spread off to the west of you. You know my spread is yonder." He jabbed his thumb in the air toward the east. "Langstons are on the other side of me. Teresa's marrying Jeff Langston."

"She's really marrying the boy next door?"

"Mom would have been thrilled." He gestured toward a pasture and filled her in on the grazing rotation patterns, then continued the tour.

At one point, Sondra turned around and gave him a quizzical look. "What?"

He'd been noticing her attire. Sondra wore that same be-draggled flannel shirt, but it managed to give her a get-down-to-business air. Her choice of footwear was another story. "You can't wear those shoes around here anymore. You need boots."

She blurted out, "I can't afford boots right now."

Dylan gave her a sardonic grin. "I'm sure Miller would want you to buy some for yourself, Sondra. *Nice* ones."

Her lips parted momentarily, then thinned. "I'll go see about the water troughs."

"I'm not finished showing you around."

She said nothing more and started walking off.

He scowled, then let out a loud sigh. "You already running scared, city-girl?"

Sondra turned and folded her arms akimbo. "I understand you're upset about Miller's will—"

"There's an understatement." His eyes narrowed.

She stared straight back at him. "We have to make this work. It's not going to be easy. Since I know how to take care of the troughs, I'll stay busy while you take care of more pressing issues."

"You got that right." He said nothing more and strode off.

❧

His tone left her steaming in the tennis shoes he disapproved of. By noon, she was a mess. It turned out they used sawdust instead of straw or hay in the stable. It supposedly absorbed better and needed changing less often—both strong points as far as she was concerned. Even then, being around as Joseph mucked out the stable nearly sent her running back out behind the barn again.

She'd scrubbed the cement water troughs herself. When she finished that chore, she slogged back to the house, shook off as much sawdust as she could, and toed out of her shoes before stepping over the threshold. Sondra hadn't engaged in anything half so strenuous in years. After indulging in a long shower, she stared at her reflection in the mirror and gave herself a much-needed pep talk. " 'I can do everything through him who gives me strength.' Yes, I can. With God's help, I can do this—even if Dylan's going to be a pain."

After hastily slapping together a peanut butter sandwich, she went back out to gather up the loose chickens and shove them back into the henhouse. One of the ranch hands, Jack, came by and gave her a little help. He then mentioned, "Nickels is in the barn. You've got a late-calving Holstein. Things ain't goin' so good."

"Oh." She paused for a second, then decided, "I'll go check to see if he needs something."

Edgar waited until he thought she was out of range and then moaned, "Lord, help us all. A meddlin' city-gal in a birthin' shed."

His low opinion of her, though deserved, nettled Sondra. She'd stay up late, read everything she could, and work twice— no, three times—as hard as they expected to prove she had what it took.

Nickels greeted her with a silent bob of his head. Other than that, he completely ignored Sondra as he ran his weathered hand over the cow's bulging side. For a few minutes, Sondra looked at the cow. She was huge. Somehow, a picture in a book made cattle look cute and of manageable size. Up close, they appeared more like odd-colored, spindle-legged fortresses. Especially pregnant, this one could pass for a small principality in Europe. Big, sad eyes rolled up at Sondra, and her heart melted. She carefully made her way across the pen and knelt by the cow's head. She petted her and murmured, "You'll be fine."

"Don't go tellin' her things are gonna be okay, ma'am. From the looks of it, they ain't," Nickels stated grimly. "Gonna have to call the vet."

"I'll do it." She went back to the house. Just as she located the vet's number, the phone rang. "Hello?"

"Mrs. Thankful, I—"

She interrupted, "Mr. Ward, I don't have time to waste listening to your innuendoes and suppositions. If that's all this is, forget it."

"I figured we ought to talk."

She shifted in the chair. "Perhaps, but you've gotten me at a bad time. At the moment, I need to call the vet."

"Why?"

"A cow is having trouble calving."

"Why didn't you call me? I'm on my way. Don't bother trying to reach the vet. He's out of town." He hung up before she could say another word.

Dylan got there in just a few minutes. He took one look at the cow and started to unbutton his shirt. Nickels spouted off any number of salient facts and made a few suggestions. Sondra didn't understand half of what he said. It irked her that Nickels became so talkative with Dylan when he'd been silent with her.

"City-girl, this is going to get ugly," Dylan warned with a lopsided, mocking smile. "You'd best scamper on back inside unless you want to lose your supper."

"I guess it's fortunate I haven't eaten supper yet."

She fought the heated blush that zoomed clear up from her toes as Dylan took off his shirt. His shoulders looked even broader without the covering of a shirt. His skin matched the color of fire-glazed pottery—tanned to the point of redness.

Dylan gave her an impatient look. She stood there, feeling completely flummoxed. "Lady, you'll need to learn to pitch in if you plan to make it through the next year," he snapped. "So, if you're staying, make yourself useful."

"What do you want?"

"Bring in six buckets of water and some soap."

By the time she hauled in the sixth bucket of water, Sondra gathered her wits enough to also bring a few towels. She watched as Dylan soaped all of the way up to his shoulder. He grimaced, then knelt down at the business end of the cow.

Feeling sympathetic, Sondra went back by the cow's head, sat cross-legged in the thin layer of sawdust covering the floor, and took hold of the rope Nickels had tied around the cow's neck. "It's okay, girl. Take it easy. Easy." She winced as she watched Dylan.

"It's malpresentation, all right. Lateral. I'll see if I can't. . . nudge. . . Nickels, brace her. I'm going to have to get some pressure going here."

With obvious skill, patience, luck, and strength, Dylan managed to turn the calf. Weak as the cow was, he ended up pulling the calf out. As he washed the worst of the mess from himself, he and Nickels discussed what remained to be done.

"Any other late calves due?"

Nickels shrugged. "One that I know of."

"I'll have my men pull down the fence tomorrow. We'll have both herds summer together for now. I'll decide the rest later."

Sondra stewed silently. Even if she didn't know diddly-squat about ranching, he owed her the courtesy of informing her about these matters before he made announcements. She didn't expect a full-on consultation, but a brief word in advance was reasonable. To her dismay, Dylan Ward didn't seem like the reasonable sort at all.

Dylan turned and gave her that mocking smile again. "You kept your stomach, city-girl. I'm surprised."

"I'm sure you'll be surprised a few more times before our year is up."

He tilted his head at the calf. "So what do you think?"

"I think it was a miracle," she said in awe.

"Don't expect too many miracles." Dylan then rasped at Nickels, "I expect to be called any time there's a problem. Don't let me find one out by accident again."

"You got it, boss."

As much as it galled her, Sondra kept her mouth shut. She didn't dare alienate her ranch hands. Miller knew his business well, and he'd hired only the best. She shouldn't make matters so uncomfortable that they'd decide to leave.

Both men were looking at her. Sondra sensed that they wanted to be rid of her. They'd been working a long while and probably missed supper, but she didn't have much of a notion what was in her kitchen. Instead of offering to rustle up a quick meal, she excused herself and bade them a good night.

Bed never felt so good and night never passed so quickly.

Her muscles protested as much as her grainy eyes did, but Sondra dragged herself out of bed at first light and hastily prepared to meet the day. She headed for the stable and used a dolly to move the hay bales to help Joseph feed the horses.

Feeling quite proud of herself, she then went to the hen-house to meet Luna. In a soft drawl, he told her all about the coop, how he cleaned and packaged eggs, and how much to feed the chickens.

Dylan sauntered up. He looked cocky—just like the class troublemaker before he pulled a stunt. Sondra got suspicious.

"I have men taking down that section of fencing. Get in the Rover, and I'll take you to see what we're doing. I have the others retagging some of the stock we purchased at auction."

"I'd like that." After seeing more of the outlying area of the ranch, she felt breathless. How could Miller have given her all of this? It amazed her. Then again, it humbled her. She now knew she wouldn't ever be equal to the task of running it. She also knew precisely why Dylan insisted on this expanded tour—he wanted to drive that fact home.

four

Sondra arrived back at the house just in time to have the Battered Women's Society take away a few pieces of the furniture. She and Kenny hadn't started out with much, but her own things were due the next day. Miller would have been glad the things she didn't need went to a good cause.

She couldn't believe how the place already felt like home. Cleaning each room, putting her things in the drawers, just angling a chair toward the window so it would catch the morning sun—each little thing made this her refuge, her haven.

Never before had a place seemed so right, so welcoming. Even her apartment with Kenny didn't feel this way. She'd barely gotten her meager belongings in the door the week they got back from their honeymoon, and they'd been so wrapped up in each other, she'd didn't cull through everything until the last week before he died. Then she hated going home because it constantly reminded her of the emptiness in her heart.

This was different. It was home—good, pure, safe— hopefully, forever.

She put her Bible and the Bible study book she'd been working through on an end table and wrapped her arms about her ribs. *Lord, thank You for providing this home for my baby and me. Grant me wisdom so I can keep it and use it to Your glory, I pray. And Father—about Dylan—help me deal with him.*

After doing some housekeeping, she drove into Lasso, stopped at the library, slipped in to see the doctor, and went through the grocery store. She located the community church and noticed Sunday morning worship started at half past eight.

Weary beyond her tolerance, she went to bed early, then barely managed to wake up in time to let the movers bring in her things. They didn't take long, but she directed them to place the furnishings exactly where she wanted them. Her tiny dinette set looked perky in the kitchen.

This was to be her son's home, and she wanted it perfect. Her child would never be passed around and suffer living without roots the way she had. He'd know the security of growing up in one house, loved. He'd have his very own bedroom, and he'd go to the same school year after year. It was a priceless gift, and Sondra could scarcely close her eyes at night, fearing she'd wake up and find it was all just a dream.

The last couple of days stayed overcast, so she'd worn loose-fitting sweats. Since today's forecast boasted sun, she put on lightweight jeans and teamed them with an oversized pink T-shirt. Feeling encouraged with her progress all around, she skipped down the steps and off to check in over at the stable. Nickels was saddling up a mare. "I'll be in the coop," she mentioned.

He shot her an approving smile. "You're not letting weeds grow 'round your feet, are you?"

"Not at all. There's too much to do!"

He nodded sagely. "Yep. Always is."

Hens clucked a welcome to her, and Sondra stepped into the coop. Luna wasn't here yet, but she wanted a chance to start in on the chores so she wouldn't be relying on others. A short while later, feeling a presence, she looked up and gave her neighbor a nod. "Mr. Ward."

❧

Finding her pitching in at barely past daybreak settled well with Dylan. "Luna's sick."

"That's too bad. Does he need anything?" She stood up and wiped the back of her wrist across her forehead. With her other hand, she cupped a little chick to her breastbone as if she'd never held anything quite so precious.

"You're already busy enough. His wife is taking care of him." Her concern threw him for a loop. Dylan liked seeing that she had some redeeming qualities. He silently reminded himself that she was a city-gal. A helpless one. The only real connection she claimed to the Curly Q was the chickens.

Swiping the chick she held and giving it a gentle buff with his knuckles, he wondered aloud, "Just how often do you take these little critters into town?" He watched as she bent over and nabbed another chick. Tenderness washed over her face as she fingered it. The look in her eyes made his heart beat a bit faster.

"Every other week. It's often enough to let the kids enjoy them, but stretched out just enough that they still think it's special. It lets them anticipate." She lifted the downy little ball and turned him so they were face-to-beak. Her voice went up half an octave. "And the kids just love you to pieces, don't they?"

The chick peeped on cue.

Sondra then cuddled it against her ribs and wet her lips. She looked Dylan in the eye and lifted her chin. The sweetness in her face disappeared, only to be replaced by cool resolve. "Since we're alone—about the boots—"

He lifted a hand to halt her. "I need to speak my piece first, if you don't mind."

The corners of her mouth tightened, and the tension he'd first felt when he entered the coop returned. Feeling rather silly to be fiddling with a handful of fluff when he planned to eat crow, Dylan passed the chick back to her. As she juggled both, he cleared his throat and remembered what he'd resolved last night as he lay awake and chafed at this whole arrangement. "I've been thinking. We've gotta make the best of things for a year. It's obvious we started off on the wrong foot."

"And started rubbing blisters," she added under her breath.

He raised his brows. This gal had gumption. "I gotta admit,

you're turning out to be a bit of a surprise. You seem like a ready-to-work woman, and you're learning mighty fast."

She carefully set down the chicks, folded her arms across her ribs, and looked at him for a long count. She had to realize Miller trapped him into a heap of hard work since she didn't have much to offer in this so-called partnership. One year of work, and he'd drag her through. . .but he figured she'd realize she wasn't cut out for this life. Then he'd buy the place at a fair price. He could tolerate the wait.

He cleared his throat. "I think it would make things go a lot better if we try to keep things on a neighborly basis."

They were both tense as just-strung clothesline. Finally, she nodded. "You've got a deal."

"Dandy." Relief flooded him. At least she didn't carry a grudge. Hardworking. Fast learning. Tenderhearted. Best he concentrate on those good qualities and show her a few of his own. "I thought maybe we could ride today. You need to see some of the rest of your land. There are parts that only have a rough fire road."

"I've never ridden before."

He groaned.

"Not to worry. I have a good sense of balance and a daredevil streak. If I'm on a calm mount, I'll manage."

"That remains to be seen." They left the coop and went to the stable. The gelding Miller left Dylan patiently waited outside. Dylan gave Pretty Boy an affectionate pat on the withers as they passed by him.

She stopped and visually measured the standardbred. "That beast is huge!"

"Not particularly. He's sturdy and reliable, though."

She got up on her tippytoes and bravely gave his gelding her hand to take her scent, then petted his mane and neck. The sight of her appreciating the gelding instead of veering away gave him hope. Maybe she wouldn't be as antsy as most greenhorns. He stood back and took in how surely she moved her slender hands and wondered if she'd take umbrage if he suggested she wear some snug jeans instead of those baggy ones so she wouldn't get rubbed raw. No. He'd just get her in a saddle and take her a short distance today. They'd barely waded into peace; the last thing he needed to do was get personal.

She pivoted around and smiled.

Dylan chuckled at her enthusiasm. "We can put you on a calm little pony. Come on." He accompanied Sondra into the cool stable to choose a mount.

The condition of the stable impressed him. It smelled of fresh sawdust. "Joseph already mucked in here today?"

"Yep." She shot him a quicksilver smile. "I even helped. I figure I need to know everything from the ground up—literally."

"Betcha you're getting sore muscles, city-girl."

"I'm doing whatever I need to get done."

A grin lit his face. For a tenderfoot, she didn't slack in the least. "So let's see you saddle Crackers. Take that saddle blanket and toss it over him."

"You got it." She let Crackers catch her scent, too. Dylan tilted his head in silent query, so she volunteered, "I took my class to the petting zoo every year. Along the way, I learned domesticated animals like to get to know their human partners."

"Horses are smart. You respect them, and they'll give you their heart."

Sondra nodded, flipped the rough blanket over the horse, and patted it for good measure. "Okay."

"The saddle now—heft it onto him. The knoblike thing is called a pommel. It goes in the front."

After she shot him an insulted glare, Sondra grabbed hold of the saddle and yanked. It didn't move an inch. She rubbed her hands on her thighs to dry them off.

Dylan stood back and watched. *Nervous*, he assessed, *but willing to try. She's not a coward.*

She shifted her feet wider apart. After she sucked in a deep breath, she gripped the saddle and jerked with all of her might. The saddle cleared the rail by a good four inches. Suddenly, Dylan slammed it back down.

Sondra wheeled around. "Why did you do that?"

He glowered at her for a solid fifteen seconds, anger gusting out with every breath. He latched onto her arm and hauled her out of the stall, away from the horse.

Sondra pulled free and stared at him with wide, wary eyes.

"Hold it right there." Dylan gritted the words as he took a determined step and backed her against the gate of the next stall. He grabbed her tiny wrists and held them together in one hand while his other fleetingly slid over her belly to confirm what he'd just seen. He let go of her and jerked back as if he'd discovered bubonic plague.

They stared at each other in shock. His impulsive action left her speechless, and he felt as amazed at his behavior as she was. For a long moment, they stood almost a yard apart in taut silence. Then the whole place shook with his bellow. "You're pregnant!"

five

"Thanks for telling me. I hadn't noticed."

"Don't you have any sense at all? You can't ride!"

"You invited me to!"

"I didn't know you were in the family way!"

She scowled at him. "Of course you did. How could you possibly miss it?"

He impatiently flailed an arm in the air. "How could I tell? You always roam around in that dumb shirt."

Her eyes shot sparks.

He glowered right back. "Trying to heft that kind of weight when you're carrying a baby is insane!" Long moments passed in tense silence. His gaze slowly dropped to her middle as he wondered aloud, "When did your husband die, anyway?"

Sondra stared straight through him.

He sucked in a noisy breath. Everything went stock-still for a moment, then Dylan grated, "That's it, isn't it? You hardly even show, and your husband died months ago. Whose baby is it, Sondra? Miller's? Is that why he left you everything?" When she didn't answer, Dylan kicked a post and smacked his Stetson on his thigh in exasperation. Slamming it on his head, he stomped out without a backward glance.

❧

Sondra turned back to work. All her life, people held low opinions of her—after all, her own parents neglected her so badly, she'd been removed from their care. If her own family felt she was worthless, why should anyone else consider her of value? She'd learned to ignore the sly looks, whispers, and pity of others. Protesting usually didn't solve the problem; it often cemented the wrong notion in folks' minds.

None of that matters. It doesn't. Christ paid the ultimate price for me. I don't have to worry what others think, because in His eyes, I'm priceless.

That night, Dylan Ward's voice seeped into her dreams and kept taunting her, *Whose baby is it? Whose?* By morning, she wanted to curl up into a tight ball, pull the covers over her head, and forget the world. She couldn't do that, though. Sondra Thankful was not a quitter. She'd do anything within her power to succeed—she had to, for her baby's sake.

It would be smart to hire a manager to help, though. Surely, Miller would understand—especially after what happened yesterday. Until she found that elusive person, though, she would keep going. If she secured someone soon, he'd get a chance to find his stride with the men and get the feel of the ranch. Then, when Dylan walked off with his share after the year was up, she wouldn't be left high and dry. With great resolve, she determined to see to the matter, then left the house to start her day as a know-nothing rancher.

She popped into the coop and swiftly filled the basket. The fear of finding another snake lurked in the back of her mind, but Sondra kept reminding herself that the hens were calm. When the snake was there, they'd been wild. Reassured with that observation, she finished the task and moved on to the stable.

Howie tipped his hat ever so slightly before resuming mucking the stalls.

Sondra tried hard to ignore the odor and turned to grab a spare shovel.

Howie swiped the shovel from her hands as his face puckered into a scowl. "You ain't got no call doin' that these days."

"I've been doing it!"

"Not anymore, you're not. Why didn't ya tell us you're in a delicate condition?"

Sondra looked down at her waist. "I can't for the life of me understand this. You're acting like I intentionally kept it a big secret, and I'm *showing!*"

"Not much. Not much at all. Coulda been that you needed to shed a few pounds."

"It's not a deadly disease. I'm a normal, healthy woman."

"Practicin' lullabies," he added hastily.

His choice of words amused her, but Sondra was careful not to hurt his feelings by laughing. "I'm not going to laze around. What can I do?"

"How 'bout"—He seemed a bit surprised she wanted to work, but he looked around to come up with something—"if I show you how to take care of the horses?"

"Great!"

"I've gotta finish up here first." *Plop.* A shovelful of muck punctuated his comment.

Sondra fought the impulse to step back a bit. The smell nearly overpowered her. "When do the eggs get picked up?"

"Couple or three times a week. To my reckonin' Chris Ratliff oughtta be by today."

"Fine." She smiled. "I'll go box up the eggs; then I'll be back to learn about the horses."

He paused and leaned on his shovel. "Think you're up to that?"

"Without a doubt."

Just as she finished readying the eggs, an old truck with "By His Hand" painted along the side pulled in to take her supply. Chris Ratliff gently set her aside and insisted on lifting the crates of eggs into the truck himself. He then surprised her by pressing a carton of milk into her arms.

"What is this for?"

"Ma'am." He gave her an assessing look and his mouth crooked into a sheepish grin. "A mother-to-be needs to be drinking plenty of milk. Dylan asked me to bring by half a gallon twice a week. More often if you say so."

Sondra laughed and waved her hand toward the pasture. "I have hundreds of cows. Not to sound ungrateful, but isn't this like taking sand to the beach?"

"No, ma'am. You're not supposed to be drinking raw milk. Most city-folk don't care for the taste of it, but even if you did, it's not pasteurized." He shook his head. "Now you let me know if you need more milk. Got that?"

"Yes, and thank you. Let me go get my purse."

He frowned at her. "We're neighbors."

"Yes, but—"

"Ma'am, you'd best talk to Dylan so's you'll get the picture. We all chip in and help each other out. Our extras go to the By His Hand food bank, but we swap goods as a matter of course. Just makes sense."

She felt awkward. "I'm sorry if I offended you."

"Dylan'll fill you in. You didn't get a garden in this year, so my family'll send over tomatoes and squash and the like."

"That sounds wonderful. When we slaughter a steer, I'll be sure to send over some beef."

A smile lit his face. "Ma'am, you just might fit in." He glanced back at her belly and nodded as if to punctuate his opinion. "Things'll turn out just fine."

She held the milk carton and stared at the back of the truck as he left. Dylan Ward, for seeming like the quintessential cowboy-of-few-words, sure didn't waste a moment before spreading gossip about her.

The chill from the carton sent her into the kitchen for a moment. As she put the milk into her refrigerator, the abundance of all she'd been given hit her. Gratitude swelled. She went back out singing "For the Beauty of the Earth." Most often, it was a Thanksgiving hymn, but it fit her mood perfectly.

She spent the balance of the day in the stable, happily rubbing saddle soap into the leather until it shone and brushing a few of the geldings and one of the mares. She chided Crackers for whipping her with a swish of his tail and giggled at the way the beasts twitched their skin to get rid of flies.

Though far more important things needed to be done, she lacked the experience to accomplish them—or the men wouldn't allow her to. She determined to pitch in with whatever tasks they wouldn't fret about and help everywhere she could. If she could free a man up to put his hands to something more pressing, she'd be satisfied. She buffed a saddle horn and nodded to herself. Yes, she was going to learn as much as she could, jump in wherever possible. This had to work out. Her son's future was riding on it.

"Howie?"

"Hmmm?"

"Why wouldn't Dylan let me ride? I thought it was okay."

"Not if you don't have a clue about what you're doing. A fall could cost you the babe you're carryin'."

She bit her lip and asked nothing more for a while. Howie whistled the same tune over and over as he repaired a harness until she finally gave him a sidelong glance. "What did Dylan tell you? About the baby and me?"

"Ward don't talk all that much. He's a closemouthed sorta man. Just said you're in a motherly way, and we'd better look out for you because. . ." His voice died off.

Her cheeks tingled with heat. "Because?"

"Well, ma'am. . ." He paused uncomfortably, then blurted, "Dylan said to look out for you because you ain't got enough sense to watch out after yourself!"

It should have been an insult, but considering the fact that she'd wondered if Dylan might have spread word that the baby was Miller's, she could only laugh.

After stopping by the coop to sneak a minute of cuddling a few chicks, she plodded back to the house. Her energy level needed a boost. Nuking and eating a frozen dinner would help. She felt too tired to do any cooking.

Sondra fussed around the house late that night. It took a lot of patience and concentration to make a place look just right. Too exhausted to stay up any longer, she eventually collapsed into bed, then regretted those late hours the next morning. Knowing she had no one to blame but herself for feeling weary, she had her morning devotions, then started off on her chores.

Edgar checked in on her at the coop and gave her a thumbs-up gesture. Heartened by that small sign of approval, she gathered the eggs and filled the feeders as she tried to decide how best to hire a manager. Even after she had one, she planned to continue to take care of the chickens. She loved scooping up the chicks and cradling them in her palm, petting their downy bodies, lifting them to brush their softness against her cheek. In those moments, she felt close to Miller again. He'd brought so much sunshine and laughter into her life with these balls of fluff.

The day already started building into a scorcher, and Sondra thought about changing into a lighter blouse after finishing here. First, though, she needed to add oyster shells to the feed. Searching around the barn, she spotted a small bag leaning against the wall next to the chicken feed. Unsure how much to use, she sat on the floor and cocked her head to read the bag. Still tired, she momentarily rested her cheek against another sack as she decided what else needed to be done.

❧

"Luna's still sick."

Her eyes shot open at the sound of Dylan's voice.

"I noticed you already took care of the chickens—any questions?"

"No, I'm just getting oyster shells. I was figuring out how much, but it's here on the label, so I'm set."

Dylan fought to keep from shuffling his boots like a naughty eight-year-old. "Ma'am, I owe you an apology."

He paused a moment when her face went a shade paler, but maybe after he cleared the air, she wouldn't look quite so. . .wary. "I don't hold with a man using his strength against a woman. The other day—well, I gave you ample cause to be scared. Not that I would ever do you any harm, but you don't know me well enough to trust me yet. I stepped way over the line, prying into your personal business, too. You can be sure from here on out, I'll keep my hands to myself and my big mouth shut."

Her head dipped, and she mumbled something that sounded vaguely like, "Thanks." Dylan figured that was the best he'd get out of her—better than he deserved.

He headed out to give the men their daily orders. When he finished, he remembered he needed to tell Sondra about the feed bill. Dylan looked around and realized he hadn't seen her come back out of the barn. He found her exactly where he'd left her—sitting on the floor, her temple resting against a green-and-white-checkered feed sack. Sleepy-eyed, she stared at her hands in her lap.

She didn't even realize he'd come close enough to touch her, so he quietly hunkered down to keep from startling her. Apparently, she'd lost track of the last twenty minutes. Dylan noted the dark circles under her eyes and her marked pallor.

He had stayed away all day yesterday in order for his temper to cool. At first, he could hardly fathom how a gent-down-to-the-sole-of-his-boots like Miller ever set aside his scruples enough to dally with a woman one-third his age. Then he admitted to himself that Sondra happened to be a stunning woman, and Miller probably didn't stand a chance against her feminine wiles. At least he now understood why Miller left the ranch to her. His child should inherit the land. The fact that he'd been generous enough to leave Dylan any land or livestock bespoke a deep level of personal regard.

Dylan used that time to face the cold, hard truth and came to accept the disappointment—after a year, he wasn't going to be able to buy the rest of the ranch. He owed it to the old man to help keep the place in prime condition until his child could take over. The years of commitment were staggering, but he'd do it for Miller.

Having arrived at that decision, getting along with Sondra ought to be easier. Certainly a working relationship between them needed to be forged. He'd offended Sondra. Now that he looked at her again, he revised his thinking once more. She seemed more like the lost-and-lonely variety. Presumably, she gravitated toward Miller in her grief, and things just kind of happened.

He felt guilty as a hound with a mouthful of chicken feathers. He'd spent the last thirty-six hours bitterly recriminating himself for how he'd treated her. He'd acted on sheer impulse and scared the daylights out of her. Dylan couldn't remember ever being so out of control, and it disgusted him that he'd frightened a small, pregnant woman. He'd never been more serious in his life than when he'd vowed he'd never do that again.

Watching her now, Dylan purposefully kept his voice low and mild. "Ma'am, if you're this miserable with morning sickness, why don't you stay in bed until a bit later?"

"I haven't had morning sickness for months," she muttered.

He shelved that piece of information to process later. For now, helping her seemed to be the priority. He'd been foolish enough to give her cause to loathe his contact. Limited to making a connection with speech, he ventured, "You're not sleeping worth a hoot, are you?"

Sondra gave him a helpless look, but she said nothing. Her defenseless expression cut him to the heart. The eloquent ache in her eyes transcended language. As if too exhausted to do or say a thing, she leaned back into the feed sack, and her eyes drifted shut.

Dylan eliminated the small space between them. "Bedtime, city-girl," he whispered in Sondra's fiery hair as he hitched her high against his chest. In just those few seconds, scorching heat burned through her shirt and his. Resting his jaw along her temple, he confirmed her fever. "Why didn't you tell me you're sick?"

six

"Not sick," Sondra muttered, "just pregnant."

"You're hot as the devil's skillet." He strode toward the door. "Luna probably gave you whatever he has."

"Just hot." Being jostled seemed to awaken her a bit. "Need to change into a cooler blouse."

"Sondra, you're burning up."

"No time to be sick. I'll just get a drink of water and—"

"Go straight to bed," Dylan cut in. "If you want, I'll even bring you a baby chick to hold."

"Don't start being nice to me now," she whispered brokenly. "Don't you dare. I can't take it."

His heart twisted. The woman in his arms was weak and small as a freshly hatched chick, and—his thoughts stalled when her baby somersaulted. Dylan felt the movement clearly to the marrow of his bones. No matter what feelings he had about getting saddled with watching her ranch and missing the chance to purchase the land he craved, he still couldn't abandon his basic protective urge.

"Put me down. I can walk. I promise I'll take a nap in a little while."

"Shush. You'll take more than a nap. You're staying in bed 'til Doc gives you an all clear."

"The doctor in town won't take care of me."

He carried her across the barnyard, and Nickels hightailed it to intercept them. "What's up?"

"Nothing," Sondra whispered faintly.

"Nothing, my foot! She's taken sick." Dylan kept right on moving. He shouldered his way into her door. Suddenly, Sondra's fingers scrabbled across his chest as she weakly tried to push away. Dylan reflexively tightened his hold.

Sondra let out a garbled, frantic, "Sick!"

That one word turned out to be a very pale warning for how violently ill she got. She'd been weak before that episode; afterward the woman was positively helpless. Dylan carried Sondra to the master bedroom, laid her on the bed, and gritted his teeth at the sight of her. The woman was just plain too thin. Dylan turned her face back to his. "Where do you keep your nighties?"

"Don't fit anymore," she quavered. "I wear Kenny's T-shirts. Second drawer."

Dylan yanked open the drawer. A dead man's shirts lay there in two neatly folded stacks. *They're just shirts.* "Here."

"Thank you." Hotter than hot, she still took the thin cotton garment from him.

Dylan left her some privacy, then stalked back in the room only long enough to take her temperature and follow it up with a glass of water. Needing to put some space between them, he went back out to the living room and plopped down on the couch as he grabbed for the phone.

It wasn't until then he noticed the stacks of boxes with a moving company's name emblazoned across them. Here and there, she'd already set out a few things. The place smelled of fresh-baked bread and lemon furniture polish. Instead of the well-worn, slightly dusty-and-rumpled look, the living room now carried a tidy, welcoming air. The woman acted like a little hen, setting up her nest.

Dylan mentally kicked himself. He should have asked his sister to round up a few neighbors to come help Sondra settle in. As soon as she got well, he'd pass the word that the little gal needed a bit of company and a helping hand to finish sprucing up the place. In spite of her feisty streak, he sensed a shyness about her. He'd nudge Teresa to help Sondra move in and make friends. She wouldn't be well enough to go to church day after tomorrow, but he'd invite her to start going to worship once she recovered. The worn-looking Bible on the end table told him her heart was in the right place.

He sighed and dialed the doctor. "Michelle? Dylan Ward. Let me talk to Doc."

"You okay, Dylan?"

"I'm fine. Listen—Sondra Thankful is sick. Probably the flu, but I don't like the way she looks."

"Isn't she the pregnant woman who came in yesterday?"

He didn't know she'd already gotten hooked up with Doc. It showed common sense and caution. "Yeah, she's in the family way."

"Sorry, Dylan. I tried to explain it to her yesterday. Doc doesn't treat pregnant women. His malpractice insurance is too high if he does."

"I'm asking him for advice about the flu, not the baby."

"He can't advise you since the patient is pregnant."

They went round and round until Dylan hung up in disgust. Then he heard Sondra stumble into the bathroom and retch. She slumped against the side of the tub afterward. "I'm okay. You can go home."

"Not a chance." Dylan lifted her and slipped her back into bed. She'd started shivering, so he tucked the sheet back up to her neck. "Let me make a few phone calls. You need to see a doctor—have him give you a quick look-see."

He ended up driving her back to her old obstetrician over an hour away. Luckily, the office was on the ground floor, because Sondra adamantly insisted upon walking in under her own steam. The receptionist jumped to her feet as soon as she spotted Sondra. "Come on in. I have an empty exam room."

Sondra shuffled toward the connecting door, and Dylan's hand shot out to twist the knob. He warned under his breath, "I'm coming back there with you. Don't you dare kick up a fuss."

Sondra's legs began to buckle. Wordlessly he scooped her up, strode forward, and laid her in the room. She'd grown even hotter during the ride, and her lethargy couldn't bode well. Bright red fever flags rode her cheeks, but otherwise, the woman was whiter than the paper on the exam table.

The doctor came in. His face puckered with concern. He peeked at something on her chart, set it aside, and drew closer to examine Sondra. Within mere minutes, he observed, "Mrs. Thankful, you've obviously contracted a nasty virus."

Sondra lay there, eyes closed, silent as a stone. Dylan wondered if she'd passed out.

The doctor continued, "You're badly dehydrated again."

Her eyes fluttered open. They were luminescent from tears and fever. "Please don't put me back in the hospital."

Back in the hospital? She'd been in the hospital already for something? Dylan scowled. This didn't sound good at all. Sondra didn't look any better than she sounded. Hopeless. That's how she looked. Her faint voice carried that tone, too.

The nurse gave her arm a compassionate stroke. "Sondra, at least there's someone at the hospital to take care of you."

Horrified by that justification, Dylan blurted out, "I'll take care of her."

❧

Much later that evening, Dylan turned off the bedroom light. He'd never seen a more pathetic sight. From the nurse's comments while they waited for a bag of IV fluid to finish draining into Sondra, Dylan gleaned she'd reached her sixth month of pregnancy. Kenny accompanied her to the doctor's office for her very first visit and impressed the nurse with how proud and attentive he'd been.

And I thought the kid was Miller's. She clings to a stupid flannel shirt—I was an idiot to ignore how deeply she loved her husband and make such an assumption. The thermometer registered her as too hot to wear one of those flannel jobs, but Dylan knew how much comfort she got from them, so he'd quietly tucked a shirt under the sheet with her when he'd gotten her back home.

She curled around it, smiled like she'd been given the key to heaven's pearly gates, and slipped right off to sleep.

On top of it all, Dylan felt a terrible sense of emptiness. He'd never once had a woman love him. Not like that. Not with all of her heart, the kind of love that went even beyond the grave. Sure, there had been girlfriends—but none of them ever came close to working out. Ken Thankful might be dead, but he'd been an incredibly lucky man to have had that kind of utter devotion.

seven

It had been a bad night. Sondra looked completely wiped out. Bless her heart, though, she'd never once complained. In fact, Dylan found her up twice and scolded her for not calling out to get help.

As the sun peeked through the window, Dylan brought her some juice and set a plate of crackers at the bedside. "Sondra, I've called my sister, Teresa. She's coming to stay with you. I think you'll like her."

She stared bleakly at the wall and nodded.

Worry speared through him. "Still feeling the baby move?"

"Yes."

"Good. Those kicks are a reminder of your husband's love."

She weakly rested a hand on her tummy. "This is all I have left. It's just him and me now."

Taking up a cool washrag, Dylan wiped her cheeks. Her skin was still hot as a branding iron. Lousy as she felt, she tried to valiantly spare him the tears filling her fever-glassy eyes. The woman deserved to bawl her eyes out. Instead, Sondra instinctively turned her face into the small comfort of the cloth and let out a shattered sigh.

Then the baby somersaulted.

The way her belly heaved and rolled beneath the sheets with the baby's actions shouldn't have amazed him. He saw pregnant animals all of the time. It was a common enough sight. But on her, it looked intimate beyond telling.

"My last little part of Kenny's love," she told herself in a whisper.

He'd been surrounded by family all his life; she had no one. Sympathy and compassion welled up. "Can't think of a better

49

gift of love than a baby."

"Thanks for saying that, Dylan. For your help, too."

He rubbed the back of his wrist against the bristles of his jaw. Instead of focusing on her loss, she concentrated on the positive. He admired that.

"I decided something."

He looked at her and waited. No telling what she was going to say.

"I'm not great at trusting people, but Miller loved and trusted you. There's no better recommendation. This ranch is a lot of work." The corners of her mouth tightened. "But you said you want to run it."

He nodded. "That's a fact."

"Then I'll rely on you instead of hiring a manager."

Her trust meant a lot. He curled his rough fingers around her small, soft hand, and stroked the back of her fingers with his thumb. "We'll do it together."

Rustling in the doorway made him jump and turn loose of her hand.

"Help's arrived." Teresa bustled into the room. "Hi, Sondra. I'm Teresa."

"She's still running a fever and weak as a kitten," Dylan reported.

"So I see. We'll turn that around in a few days' time," Teresa decided crisply as she nudged him to the side and grabbed the glass of juice. "So is that a boy or a girl you're carrying, Sondra?"

"A boy."

"Isn't that nice?" Teresa's hand dove under Sondra's shoulders and lifted her head. "A ranch is the ideal place for children to grow up. When are you due?"

"September second." Sondra sipped the juice. "Thanks."

"September second," Teresa echoed.

Patting her tummy weakly, Sondra added, "This is Oklahoma, baby. Folks call us Sooners, and if you take a mind to come out sooner than September, I won't complain."

Dylan chuckled as he stretched. "I need to get going. The day's already half over."

"It sure is," Teresa teased. She glanced at the clock and declared, "It's already a quarter past six! The day's half done." He playfully nudged his sister's hip with his own. "Just because you keep me from starving isn't an excuse to be sarcastic."

"I put a pan of cinnamon buns on the kitchen counter. Have a few."

"Nothing doing. I'm eating every last one of 'em."

"Impossible. Nickels and Joseph saw me bring them in. I already gave them each a pair. Bet you they take some out for Howie and Edgar, too."

"Then you're disowned."

"Teresa, I'll adopt you!"

Dylan shook his finger at Sondra. "You keep your paws off of my relatives!"

"You just disowned her!"

"He does that once or twice a week. I just don't listen." Teresa laughed. She urged Sondra to drink more, then added, "He doesn't listen to me any better."

"Sounds like plenty of the brothers and sisters I know," Sondra quipped.

"Marriages, too," Teresa tacked on.

"I'm out of here!" Dylan boomed as he turned and fled.

Teresa went into gales of laughter. "My brother is marriage-shy. Nothing gets rid of him faster than bringing up the topic of matrimony."

❧

Three days later, Sondra dragged herself out of bed. She took a shower and felt weak enough to whirl down the drain with the water.

"What are you doin' outta bed?" Nickels demanded as she passed by him out in the yard.

"I'm doing my chores. Did that last cow ever drop her calf?"

He avoided her gaze. "That's taken care of."

"Oh?"

His mouth pulled downward, and he scuffed a boot in the dirt. "Take my word for it, ma'am. It's all done."

"And mother and calf? How are they?"

His face twisted. "Ma'am, you don't want to ask 'bout this. Take my word for it."

She took a deep breath and let it out slowly. "All right. I'm going to gather the eggs."

"Dylan ain't gonna like that, ma'am. He said you're too sick to lift a finger. One glimpse of you backs up the notion, too."

"Nonsense."

The egg basket shouldn't be heavy, but it felt like a block of cement. The world tilted a bit each time Sondra got up and down, and finally she felt too dizzy to continue. Deciding a breath of fresh air would cure her, she went to the door of the coop and froze. Nickels and Dylan stood close by, holding a whispered conversation.

"Dylan, Sondra asked 'bout that last calving. I put her off."

"Good. Wait—what do you mean? Is she out of bed?"

"Yep," Nickels hissed, "and she looks plumb awful."

"One stillbirth is bad enough. The last thing she needs to do is have one herself. Stubborn woman!"

Stillbirth? The word made her reel.

Dylan's voice rose in volume, "Where is she? I'm going to tie her to the bedpost if I have to!"

"I saw her heading for the coop."

"If she isn't out cold on the floor, it'll be a miracle."

Sondra secretly smiled at his worried tone of voice. In spite of his disappointments and heavier workload, Dylan Ward cared about her. Dylan did precisely what Miller expected: He shouldered responsibilities and showed true cowboy gallantry.

Sondra smiled to herself. Dear, sweet Miller willed her this place and provided help in the form of a black-haired, gruff-voiced, softhearted rancher—sort of an angel in batwing chaps.

It would be a mistake to walk out into the middle of their conversation, but she didn't dare stay in the henhouse and wait for Dylan to stomp in and chew her out. Sondra managed to give a fair rendition of a muffled cough and walked out into the sunlight. She manufactured a tentative smile. "My body's not quite as strong as my will. Could I trouble you to please finish crating up the eggs?"

"I'll get it," Nickels volunteered. He turned sideways and sidled past her, though he and another man could have walked abreast past her with room to spare.

Dylan hooked a thumb in a belt loop, scanned her up and down, and drawled, "Woman, you have a habit of biting off more than you can chew."

"Probably."

"You're still as pasty as a plucked chicken."

Sondra leaned against the doorjamb. "I'm a bit plumper."

"Not by much." He absently shook his head and twitched a self-conscious smile. "I probably ought to apologize. That sounded a mite bit personal."

Laughter colored her voice. "Don't bother. I've been plucked, so you can't ruffle my feathers!"

Dylan started to chuckle. The rich sound filled the barnyard and made something deep inside her glow. During those moments, he looked ten years younger. His loose, leggy stride brought him to her. Without a word, he slipped his arm around her waist and started back toward the house. "Feathers," he repeated, as if it were the best joke he'd heard in ages.

His strength seeped into her. She offered, "I know chickens don't drink soda, but this one happens to have a variety of them in the fridge. You're welcome anytime."

"I'll keep that in mind. At the moment, I'm more concerned with you staying hydrated."

"I'm a big girl. I can take care of myself."

"In a pig's eye." He crooked another of those smiles. "You may as well be warned: Everyone is going to boss you around unmercifully for the next few months."

"Aren't there other women for them to nag?"

"Can't rightly say. You already discovered that Doc won't take care of you. It's not just you, either. BobbyJo Lintz up and moved back to Galveston to stay with her folks until she has her baby. Greg sent her there, but he's climbing the walls. Other than her, you're the community's only mother-to-be."

"Is that your way of telling me that I've suddenly become community property?"

"Yes, ma'am, it means precisely that." His hold tightened as they mounted the porch steps.

Trying to ignore how much she needed his support, she asked, "How is it the citizens all want to have a say when the town doctor won't speak a word to me?"

"That's a good question." He leaned forward slightly and opened the door.

She stepped inside, looked at all of the boxes, and grimaced. "This mess is awful."

"You're not doing a blessed thing other than to laze in bed. Do I need to phone Teresa and ask her to come sit on top of you?"

Teresa's voice sounded from the living room. "I'd crush the poor gal! I invited myself over because I thought Sondra might be going a little stir crazy. I'm trying my best to fix this rip in the sofa. The movers must—"

"No!" Sondra tried to wrestle free from Dylan. "No! Don't!"

Dylan's hold tightened and he rumbled, "Settle down."

"Don't let her do it!" She twisted from Dylan toward Teresa. "I don't want it fixed!"

Dylan strode around to Teresa's side and looked at a five-inch gash in the fabric. "Sondra, it needs stitching."

"No!"

Teresa frowned. "Why not?"

"Kenny did it." She knelt on the carpeting. Reaching out, she tentatively touched the slit. "His footrest had a rough spot."

Dylan and Teresa exchanged puzzled looks and echoed, "Footrest?"

"On his wheelchair."

Teresa crouched down and cocked her head. "I'll bet he'd want it to get fixed up."

"I know," Sondra whispered thickly. "But he did it right before he left our place. It was the last time I ever saw him, and I was so mad. . . ."

Dylan hunkered down on the other side of her and tilted her face to his. "No man worth his salt would want you punishing yourself like this, Sondra. So what if you had a spat? You would have made up, too. Let go of this. Patch it up, just like you would have patched up the fight."

"That's sound advice," Teresa concurred. "Do you want to sew it up, or do you want me to do it while you sit there?"

Dylan still hadn't let go of her. Sondra rasped, "I need to do it myself."

"Okay. Afterward, you go on in and take a nap."

"What about your soda?"

Dylan smiled softly. "I'll claim it some other time."

eight

Two days later, Dylan banged on the back door. When Sondra opened it, he dusted his hands off on the thighs of his jeans. "Is that offer for a soda still open?"

"Sure. Come on in."

"I'd rather sit out here, if you don't mind. I'm gritty as a gopher hole."

She opened the refrigerator, took out two cans, and went to the sink. A few seconds later, Sondra nudged him a bit so she could sit beside him on the porch steps. He tipped back his Stetson, rolled the can very slowly across his forehead, and sighed with the pleasure of that simple act. Sondra chortled softly as she handed him a wet dishcloth. "This is almost as cool."

"Mmmm. Thanks."

While he swiped at his hands, face, and neck, she popped open the tab on his soda. He accepted it with a grateful nod. "Did you and Teresa have fun today?"

"Oh, yes. Your sister is terrific with kids." He'd called her each evening to see how she fared, and he'd about had a fit last night when she let slip that she'd be going to the foster home today. Next thing she knew, Teresa invited herself to go along. They'd had a wonderful time.

"Yeah, well, she said the same thing about you." He took another gulp and swallowed it.

"If I were in a more stable situation, I'd be tempted to scoop up half a dozen of those kids and bring them home."

He gave her an alarmed look. "You wouldn't—"

She shook her head. "No. I'm already in over my head. Still, I love children. I sit them in a circle and let each one hold a chick. You should see how the kids respond. It's delightful."

He tilted the can at her. "It's delightful what it does for you."

His observation made her feel unaccountably shy. During the time she'd been sick, they'd crossed over from being unwilling partners to fledgling friends. He'd proven himself trustworthy. Since then, the aching loneliness she'd felt since Kenny's death seemed less intense.

Unaware of her musings, Dylan said, "Yep." He took another healthy swig. "It's easy to see why Miller kept the henhouse. You beam when you leave here with those chicks, and you come back aglow. Not many women find contentment with such simple pleasures."

She shrugged self-consciously. "I've never been like other gals." Uncomfortable, she quickly changed the subject. "I have hot dogs and corn on the cob in the house. Are you hungry?"

"Starving!"

He said it with such gusto, she smiled. "What do you like on your dogs?"

"Ketchup, mustard, and pickle relish."

"No onions or cheese?"

He chugged down the soda and let out a long, slow, noisy breath of bliss. "You really do 'em up. No onions. Cheese, if you have it." He then hitched a shoulder. "Sondra, I'm sweaty, hot, and real hungry. Maybe you'd rather—"

"I left a few of Miller's shirts hanging in the guest room. You're welcome to go have a quick shower. As much time as you spend here, it'd probably be a good idea for you to bring over a change of clothing. I'll eat one hot dog, maybe two. The rest are going to go rotten before I eat them again, and the buns go stale in this heat. Feel free to polish off as many as you want."

"You don't know what you're asking for."

Sondra did know what she was asking for. She hadn't shared a meal with anyone in ages. If she wanted, she could attribute feeding him to good manners and basic gratitude, but the truth of the matter was, she wanted company, and Dylan propped open the door of friendship by dropping in for a drink.

For the first time, they shared a meal. Sondra folded her hands in her lap and dipped her head for a quick, silent prayer. To her surprise, Dylan immediately started, "Heavenly Father, we give You thanks for Your grace and mercy, for Your bounty and care."

Afterward, he cleared his throat. "I guess I should have asked. It was presumptuous for me to dive in like that in your home."

"Oh, no! It was lovely. I only wish I'd made a real meal instead—"

"Hold it right there." He gave her an outraged look. "Hot dogs are an all-American meal, and I'm dead serious when I give thanks for them."

Half an hour later, Sondra asked, "How does ice cream sound?"

Dylan's eyes lit up. "Only if you eat a whole bowl full. You're still too skinny."

Glancing down at her tummy, Sondra refuted, "I'm not skinny. I've probably put on an inch a week this last month!"

"What does the doctor say about that?"

Sondra waggled her finger at him. "I knew you put your sister up to that! She just happened to know where the doctor's office was, and they just happened to slip me in for a quick check-up so the chicks wouldn't overheat in the car."

"Hey, I'm not denying it. Since you were in town, it made sense for you to see the doc. So what did he say?"

"Believe it or not, even with being sick, I gained weight this time." She grinned. "Must have been the great care my neighbors gave me."

"You're like one of those women from olden days. I'll bet my hands could about span your waist."

"That's not saying much. You have huge hands. This baby isn't staying little, either."

Dylan strove to keep a casual pitch to his voice. "What did the doc say?"

"The obstetrician said he looks fine. Everything is right on schedule, including the fact that the baby is getting the hiccups."

"They really don't—do they?"

"Oh, yes. The rascal bumps up and down like he's on a teeter-totter."

"I still don't believe it. If he does it when I'm around, you let me know."

Sondra gave him a wary look. "Why?"

A wave of awkwardness swelled. Dylan shifted and groused. "Because. . .awww, just forget it. Skip the ice cream. I need to get going."

"I love rocky road. That and fudge brownie. There's always one or the other in the freezer, and I'll keep soda in the fridge. You're welcome to help yourself anytime." She dipped her head and wondered what made her blurt that out. His quick wit and easygoing nature made him fun to be around. Though she'd surprised herself with that invitation, she meant every word of it.

Shuffling his weight from his left boot to his right, Dylan stood at the door, plunked his Stetson on and rumbled, "You strike me as woman who values her privacy. I don't imagine I'll claim those much."

She looked directly at him. "I'm not the type to make empty gestures. Some women are good at coy games and small talk. Me?" She flicked him a strained smile. "I got shuffled around in the system too much to ever get good at those social conventions. You can take whatever I say at face value, so don't feel shy about popping in the back door if you're thirsty."

"I'll keep that in mind." He left.

Sondra stared at the door and wondered what had gotten into her. The only other men she'd ever felt that way with were Kenny and Miller. That fact jarred her.

Still, she went to the refrigerator and rearranged things. . . just so the soda cans would be up front. After all, what were partners for?

❧

She made it through her seventh month of pregnancy quite nicely. The hands wouldn't let her do much of anything. They gave her tummy assessing looks and nudged her out of the way. Gathering eggs, helping groom the horses, and feeding the dogs and cats were her chores. She quickly mastered the software on Miller's computer so she could keep track of orders, bills, and payroll. Every other Friday, she passed paychecks out to the hands and thanked them wholeheartedly for their labor.

Since they wouldn't hear of her doing many of the ranching chores, Sondra made it a practice to bake something a couple times a week. The men cooked for themselves at the bunkhouse, but they definitely appreciated having her desserts. She soon learned Howie liked pie of any variety, Nickels shared her weakness for chocolate, and Frank didn't care what it was as long as it was sweet. Edgar liked apples in his things, while Joseph could eat an entire batch of cookies all by himself. With those preferences in mind, she tried to rotate her choices.

It wasn't long before she ran into one of the men from Dylan's spread at the grocery store. Scanning the flour and butter in her cart, he drawled, "Heard tell you make a mean apple pie."

Her lips parted in surprise. Folks in this small town were astonishingly friendly. Men and women she'd never met chatted with her at the store or on the sidewalk. They invariably asked about Dylan, too. She wasn't comfortable talking about herself, and she had no idea what to say about him other than to mention he was a hardworking man. That always garnered a nod of agreement.

Dylan's ranch hand grinned. "Edgar came over. He and Dylan planned tomorrow."

Sondra still didn't see the connection.

"Edgar told Dylan they'd save him a slice of your pie. Said you just put a couple in the bunkhouse."

"Oh." She wrinkled her nose. "What's happening tomorrow?"

"We're going to cull the herds and sell off some beef. Dylan has Teresa making barbecue afterward."

"Why hasn't Teresa called me?"

"Ma'am, I never pretended to be able to read a woman's mind."

She barely quelled her laugh. "Can you read a man's?"

"Every once in a while. Mostly when he's lookin' at a woman or something good to eat."

"That doesn't take much skill," Sondra decided with mock solemnity. "It's a good thing you're a decent cowboy."

He gave her a slow smile and shook his head. "You know, Dylan's right. That spunk of yours might get you through this."

Sondra smiled and pushed her cart down the next aisle. She cruised to the produce section again to pick up more apples.

The next day, Sondra called Teresa. At four thirty, she showed up at Dylan's ranch, the Laughingstock. Teresa helped her transfer five apple pies, a chocolate cake, potato salad, and six dozen homemade rolls from her car to the picnic tables. She made lemonade as Teresa filled her in on snippets of news.

The air was redolent with the heady aroma of roasting beef when the men sauntered over. Soon as Dylan asked grace, a solid dozen men attacked the table. "Hey! Sondra made pie!"

"That's dessert!" Teresa shouted. "You leatherhands leave it be 'til you've eaten everything else."

"Whoa! Them rolls ain't store-bought."

"Pitch me a couple!"

Dylan paced up to Sondra. She turned away and fussed to keep napkins from blowing away. She didn't want to look at him. He made her breath hitch.

Due to being in a wheelchair, Kenny had boasted impressive chest and arm muscles. Dylan, though—on him, those corded muscles spoke of heavy labor and the ability to tackle any task. He walked with rugged assurance, and every inch of him shouted masculine confidence. He'd easily held and carried her—and that somehow suddenly seemed significant. *What am I doing even looking at him?*

Unaware of his effect on her, Dylan arrived at her side with a heaping plate of beef in his hands. He extended it to her. "You'd best elbow in and get some of that food or these hogs'll inhale it all in five minutes flat."

Sondra shook her head. "I can't eat a fraction of this."

"That's nothing!"

"It's too much, seeing as I have a passenger on board. Plain and simple, there's just not enough room."

"That passenger needs good nutrition. How much milk are you drinking? What about fruits and vegetables?"

"Dylan, I'm a grown woman. I don't need you to hover."

"How much weight have you gained?"

Her jaw dropped.

"Well?"

"That's none of your business!"

He grabbed her arm. "Make way, guys. Sondra needs to eat up."

"Stop this!" she hissed.

"Give her a roll. They taste mighty fine."

"You knothead! She made 'em," Edgar announced.

Dylan paused for a second and looked at her. "You're supposed to be resting. You made the pies. What were you thinking, making rolls, too?"

"If you're going to give her the business, best you do it up right," the man behind her tattled. "She made that there potato salad and the chocolate cake, too." He then tugged on Sondra's maternity smock. "If he fires me, I expect a job on your spread."

"Are you kidding? You've just gotten the man so mad at me, I'm mincemeat! All I owe you is indigestion!" She set her plate down. "I already have a good enough case of it to last both of us!"

"It's no wonder. You push yourself too hard and don't eat right," Dylan snapped. "This kid is going to be a sickly little thing if you don't start filling up with decent grub. When's the last time you ate liver?"

Momentarily closing her eyes in horror, she shuddered. "Liver?"

"You heard me right. Liver. For iron."

"I take an iron tablet."

"Not good enough. You don't get all you need from a stinking, little artificial pill. Quit stalling. When's the last time you had liver? Last week? Two weeks ago?" When she shook her head, he growled threateningly, "Last month?"

"Kindergarten."

"That does it!" He raised his voice, "Teresa, where's the liver from this beast? Fix it up right quick. Sondra needs to eat it."

Sondra shook her head. "I won't."

"Yes, you will. Your son deserves it."

"What did he ever do to you?"

Dylan gave her a disapproving look.

Pressing her hand over her stomach, Sondra complained, "You're making my indigestion even worse, so stop scowling at me."

"We'll walk you."

She gave him an incredulous look. "Walk me?"

Nodding curtly, as if he'd come to some momentous decision and solved the entire problem, Dylan informed her, "Walking. Until your colic passes. It works great for horses."

Sondra turned away, and everyone glared at him. *Now what did I do wrong?* Suddenly his eyes widened and he stepped back, but the table stopped him. "Sond—" A perfectly good apple pie hit his face.

nine

Her phone jangled incessantly for the next hour. Sondra finally unplugged it. She curled up in bed and stewed. How dare Dylan treat her like that? *A horse!*

Mixed in with her anger was a dawning sense of embarrassment. She'd actually hit Dylan with a pie—took the tin and smeared the whole thing all over his face. He must be absolutely livid. She'd humiliated him in front of all of his men.

He was clueless. I overreacted. She lay in the dark and winced. Apologizing to him wouldn't be easy, but she owed him that much. In fact, nothing would ever cancel the debt she owed him. Yes, he'd get land and livestock at the end of the year. . . but he'd earn it.

One thing for sure: Dylan needed the land. Wisely enough, he'd refrained from repeating his desire to have first bid at the remainder of the ranch after the year lapsed. He was doing the nearly impossible, running two ranches. She appreciated it, but at the same time, on nights like tonight, Sondra was reminded it wasn't an altruistic gesture. He helped her because of what he'd get in the end.

Doing the books let her plainly see what the value of the cattle would be, come reckoning time. Then, too, Mr. Cheviot had advised her to get the land appraised so she could adequately deduct it from the property tax when it came due. Dylan was putting in hard work—but in the end, he would walk away with a very handsome reward. If he failed, he was no worse off—but she'd lose her home, her dreams, and the future she wanted for her son.

From the day she moved in, she'd never considered that tract of land or portion of cattle hers. Miller dangled it in front of Dylan to ensure his capable assistance. Sondra wanted him to succeed—not only so she'd be able to stay, but also because Dylan worked with incredible diligence. He deserved what Miller bequeathed him.

But then why is he fretting over the baby?

The next morning, Sondra fumbled to open her car door. She needed to go apologize.

"Ain't gonna open unless you unlock it," Edgar drawled.

Sondra's face twisted in chagrin as she realized she'd locked her keys in the car. Her moan brought Edgar closer.

"Don't get yourself in a tizzy. It's no big deal." Edgar whistled and waved. Chris Ratliff pulled up. "Perfect timing. The lady's locked herself out. How's about you helping her?"

"No problem." Chris pulled a metal strip from beneath the front seat of a battered-looking green work truck. Seconds later, he opened Sondra's door with a flourish.

"How'd you do that?" She gaped at him.

"I repair cars for a living. It would be too embarrassing to call up customers and tell them I locked myself out of their cars."

Sondra ventured, "If I made both of you your very own treat, would that suffice as hush money?"

"No need to," Chris said.

Grinning from ear to ear, Edgar shook his head. "Ma'am, if you'd offered that yesterday, I'd take you up on it in a hot second. I can't now."

Dread iced down her spine. "Just what do you mean?"

"I can't rightly say." He rubbed the back of his neck and looked guilty as sin.

Chris chuckled and drove toward Nickels to pick up the eggs.

"Edgar—"

Her steely tone seemed to amuse him. "You may well be mad at me, but I'd rather suffer your wrath than Dylan's any day. 'Specially since I've tasted your pies."

"Argh!" she said theatrically. She may as well make fun of herself. "I have a sneaking suspicion I'm never going to live that down."

He thumbed his hat back a tad. "Now that's probably a fact."

Rats.

"Then again, good as I heard tell the other pies were, I suspect we're all gonna hold Dylan to blame for costing us one."

Sondra laughed at his hangdog expression. "Didn't you get a slice?"

"Mournful fact is I barely got a taste."

"I see. Give me a day or so, and I'll make it up to you."

His eyes locked in on her belly. "I'd be much obliged, but I'm not sure you ought to be going to such trouble."

"It's no trouble. I like being in a kitchen."

He shook his head. "Never did see me a woman who kept as busy as you do. Suspect it has to do with you being on the nest, so to speak. Between you peekin' and peckin' into everything 'round the ranch and Dylan gettin' antsy 'bout trying to tie you down, a body could be rightfully entertained."

"The show's over for today." She scooched behind the wheel and headed toward Dylan's spread. LAUGHINGSTOCK, proclaimed the sign over the gate. Sondra winced. *That's me, all right. I've managed to let go of my temper and make a fool of myself.*

One of Dylan's men said he wasn't there, and he didn't know where to find him. Sondra thought about calling him, but she wanted to apologize in person. Driving on, she went to Lawton and parked at the first store she found. After a month and a half of poring over the computer and tending to bills, Sondra knew full well that her financial state might be characterized as exceedingly stable. As a matter of fact, she'd never imagined that Miller Quintain possessed such staggering wealth. Though she didn't particularly want anything for herself, she knew the time had come to buy things for the baby.

≥a

Accustomed to the sight of Sondra traipsing around with a couple of the hounds scrambling at her feet, Dylan missed seeing her that morning. Pressing business matters forced him away from the ranches until noon.

Last night, he'd tried to call her to apologize, but she wouldn't answer the phone. He'd gotten an earful from every man at the barbecue—they'd been ready to beat him to a bloody pulp. As if the men hadn't been voluble enough, his sister nearly smacked him. "What got in to you? The poor gal! A horse? Walk her like a horse?"

He clamped his big mouth shut.

"I can't believe you compared Sondra to a horse." She shook her head. "Go clean up. Afterward, you'd best crawl over there on your hands and knees and apologize!"

He barked defensively, "All I was trying to do was get her to eat better. How is a bachelor supposed to know what a pregnant widow does for indigestion?"

Howie piped up. "She's been keepin' a bottle of antacid tablets in the stable."

Dylan nearly exploded. "Anything you know about her comes directly to me, do you hear that? Anything. Miller put her in my care. The last thing I need is for the lot of you to go leavin' me in the dark about the particulars."

Someone grumbled, "She's an adult. She takes pretty good care of herself."

"You can't be serious! She hasn't had liver even once. Every fool knows she supposed to eat liver. And when she got sick—remember when she got sick?"

Nickels admitted, "She was pitiful."

Teresa rubbed her hands on a napkin. "Enough's been said. I doubt Sondra would appreciate being the topic of any further conversation. Just do your best by her."

Dylan held up a hand and added, "And each of you comes to me with anything—otherwise, you'll be looking for work elsewhere. Any questions?"

No one said a thing.

Still, his message got through. As soon as he showed up that afternoon, Edgar reported, "Miz Sondra locked herself out of her car today. Went shoppin', too. Brung back loads of baby stuff. She's up at the house."

Armed with a carton of rocky road ice cream as a peace offering, Dylan headed for her door. She didn't answer his knock. He wasn't sure whether she refused to speak to him or if she was in trouble. He knocked once more. With no response, he decided to take her at her word. Dylan opened the kitchen door. He strode into the kitchen, letting his boots scrape on the floor loudly in hopes she'd call out a howdy. She didn't.

He stuck the ice cream in her freezer, expecting she'd hear him and make an appearance. When she didn't, he peeked into the empty living room. Maybe in the basement—doing laundry perhaps? Nope. The light was off down there. Her bedroom was empty, too. His heart started to race.

A soft sound made him push open the last door. Dylan stood there and tilted his head to the side. His eyes narrowed. Asleep? In here? He drew closer and confirmed his suspicion. She looked vulnerable as she slept. Her lashes fanned across her cheekbones and fluttered a little. Her lips pouted. He winced at how kissable she looked.

Whoa. Where did that thought come from? For all of its surprise, the admission rang true.

She had no right to look so adorable. And cuddly. Peach and yellow flowers dotted the dress that draped her softer, fuller curves. Sondra had gained some weight—enough to fill in the hollows of her cheeks pleasantly, and the radiance of her skin brought to mind the cliché of how pregnant women glowed.

Oh, man. I'm getting lassoed by my own rope.

She favored some heady perfume—an exotic blend of subtle spices and a hint of flowers that left him inhaling deeply after she walked past. Just a whiff, and he'd hold his breath to appreciate the scent a moment longer. The intelligent sparkle in her eye captivated him. And the way she sometimes pursed her lips as she thought or absorbed something he told her—as if she were ready for a kiss.

Oh, he'd been appreciating the sight all along. Truth be told, she'd slowly been driving him crazy—but until this moment, he'd attributed it more to obligation and her quirky nature. Never once had he admitted his heart might be getting involved.

Through it all, he'd been sort of a neutral party. Exhibiting a polite modicum of concern and a proprietary interest were all that seemed appropriate. After all, they were partners of a sort. Miller had entrusted her into his care.

Besides, she was a widow. Carrying another man's baby. And he was a Christian brother. That certainly put him in a position of helping out.

Until now. Just as soon as Dylan admitted to himself that he'd fallen, and fallen hard, the sucker punch came. He could want her from now 'til the moon fell out of the sky, but wanting didn't matter when it was one-sided. Then, too, he didn't cotton to the notion that he would be last in line. Sondra's world revolved around the child she carried. That was admirable. . .but it also pointed out a glaring fact: That baby would always bind her heart to Kenny.

She cherished her memories of Kenny—and though that was well and good, he'd once been a mortal man. . .but Dylan knew he'd now be competing with saintly memories. That went over about as well as getting bucked off into a cactus patch. Nope. He shook his head. Partners. Brother and sister in Christ. That's all he and Sondra would ever be.

Other than when she had the flu, she'd been bouncing

around and getting into everything. Indigestion might be a bit of a nuisance, but overall, she'd never complained or shied away from doing anything. Leave it to a sassy woman like her to carry a kid with confidence. She didn't want or need special considerations.

Just then, the baby moved, making the flowered fabric of her dress ripple in the most fascinating way. Dylan watched in silence. It was such an amazing sight. A little frog-catching, jackrabbit-chasing, cowlick-headed boy was inside of her. What a wonder!

Tension sang through every last inch of her. His eyes narrowed. "You're awake."

She let out a cry.

ten

"Hey, settle down," Dylan placated in a soft tone. "It's just me. Everything's okay. I brought some ice cream. Rocky road."

Sondra wet her lips and nodded slowly. She sat on the far side of the bed, back pressed against the wall. Her eyes were huge.

Stuffing his hands in his pockets, Dylan realized aloud, "I spooked you. I'm sorry."

" 'S okay."

"Not really. You look like you wanna scream. I'll go dish up ice cream. Okay?" He headed for the kitchen and decided to have a bowl, too. A relaxed time together was just the ticket—and no one could get het-up mad while eating ice cream. He scooped out several hunks and created a mountain in each bowl.

"Dylan! What army is going to help me do that justice?"

He turned. "You're on your own." Grinning wasn't hard. She'd run a comb through her hair so it fell in a fiery, bouncy fall past her shoulders. Her flowered dress looked springy and cool.

Self-consciously smoothing out a few wrinkles over her tummy, Sondra said, "I should have changed."

"You look cuter than a bug's ear. Come sit down." Thumping the bowls onto the table, Dylan waggled his brows. "I brought your favorite."

She sat, took up her spoon, and let out a small sigh of pleasure as she swallowed her first bite. A moment later, she frowned at her hand. "My ring's getting tight."

"Better take it off."

She chewed on her lip and shrugged.

He wondered if it was already stuck. Forcing himself to not look at her hand took considerable self-control. He'd already blundered by giving his opinion about how she ought to take care of herself. A pregnant widow had every reason to want to keep on her wedding band. Still, she needed to be sensible. "When you're ready, a little butter might make it slip off a bit easier."

"I'll keep that in mind. I thought maybe bag balm would do the trick."

He shot her a quirky smile. "Ma'am, you said it, I didn't."

She wrinkled her nose. "Dylan, I owe you an apology. I let my hormones and temper get ahead of me last night—"

"I owe you an apology," he interrupted. He searched for the right words, "About the—"

"How about we both forget that unfortunate episode?"

He started to chuckle. "You're not hearing me complain. Your revenge was mighty sweet."

She smiled as she took a bite of ice cream.

He finally allowed himself to look at her left hand. "Ma'am, if your band gets much tighter, you'll be in trouble—but then again, I've proven myself to be wholly ignorant regarding maternity and women, in general. I'll have to beg your pardon if I get a mite jumpy about you. . ." He waved his spoon toward her tummy. "And all of this."

"There's nothing to fret about. Overall, I've been very lucky. Six weeks to go, and I'm feeling fine." She looked pleased—though he wasn't sure whether her relief came from the fact that she was so close to the end of being in a family way, or that they'd dropped the subject of her ring.

"When are you going to move into the city?"

Her spoon clattered to the table. "I'm not moving!"

"Oh, come on, Sondra! I wasn't talking about you leaving permanently."

"I'm staying right here."

"You have to be closer to medical care for when the baby

comes. No one's gonna take that as abandonment. Other mothers-to-be do it. As a matter of fact, BobbyJo Lintz just came back home yesterday after having their kid."

"Really? What did she have?"

"A boy. Your youngster will have a pal on the school bus. Nice, eh?"

Sondra glowed. "Wonderful! I'll have to make her a few meals."

"Oh, no, you don't! What you need to do is settle down and rest."

"I was lying down."

"After you went roaming all over creation. I saw all of those shopping bags."

"Those are a few essentials. I'm going to order the nursery furniture from Nielson's."

He nodded. Sondra showed good judgment, buying big-ticket items from a local family who also happened to worship at their church. She'd adjusted to small-town living like the proverbial duck to water. Rubbing his hand across his jaw, Dylan blurted out, "Are you sure the baby's healthy?"

"There aren't any guarantees, Dylan. So far, things look fine."

"Why was your husband in a wheelchair? I mean, was it because of a birth defect?"

"Motorcycle accident."

"Before or after you got married? Aw, forget I asked. It's none of my business."

Sondra licked a dot of chocolate off her lower lip and shook her head. "No one's asked me about Kenny since he died. It's spooky—like I'm supposed to pretend he never existed or anything. I loved him. I don't want to forget him."

"Makes sense." Dylan stared at the ice cream melting in his own bowl. The last thing he wanted to hear was how much she loved another man—even if Kenny was dead.

"Ken and I met at a coworker's birthday bash. He and I hit

it off right away. I'd sprained my ankle and had to camp out on the couch. We ended up talking for hours."

"He must have had the time of his life."

"I sure did. I'm a sucker for a man in jeans and a flannel shirt."

"Hmm. You're in trouble." *And I'm in luck. I live in jeans and flannel shirts all winter.*

"Why am I in trouble?" Her brows rose. "Because the men around here wear them?"

When he nodded, she shrugged. "I don't think that'll be much of an issue. I'll be far too distracted to care about anyone who doesn't wear a diaper."

Dylan shifted uncomfortably. "Ah, Sondra?"

"Yes?"

"You're a pretty little gal. You've got a bunch of money and a fine ranch. I hope you'll be careful. Plenty of slick guys would be more than happy to slip in and get their hands on such a deal."

"Mr. Cheviot warned me of the same thing when I signed the papers. I'm not worried, Dylan. It's nice of you to be concerned, but I don't think I'm heart-whole enough to think about loving anyone again."

Some things can't be hurried. I'll give you time, honey.

She stared at the melting ice cream in her dish and his empty bowl. She made a ragged attempt to clear her throat. "I hate being a crybaby."

Dylan rose and stood by her. He skimmed his big hand up and down her back. "You're not being a crybaby. You're just a woman with too many responsibilities and a broken heart." He smoothed her hair as she took a few deep breaths to calm herself. "A man would be lucky to be loved the way you loved Ken."

"Don't you have someone, Dylan?"

"No. Miller must have eaten locoweed when he stuck that option in the will about us getting married. Bad enough he got that bee in his bonnet. Even worse, Teresa nearly drives me crazy with her matchmaking schemes. Our folks were one of those rare couples who were madly in love with each other. Teresa's engaged to Jeff Langston, and they're both disgustingly happy together. I couldn't be more pleased for them."

"With that kind of example, why haven't you taken the plunge?"

He shrugged. "I'm waiting on God's timing."

"The loneliness is awful, isn't it?"

"I'm not complaining." He intentionally kept his voice light. The last thing she needed was for him to underscore the emptiness of solitary nights and meals for one. He gave her a playful pat. "Eat the rest of your ice cream."

"I'm full."

"Want me to make you eat liver instead?"

&

Dylan finished putting the chicks back with the hens. Sondra still took them to the group home for foster kids every other week. He didn't cotton to her driving that far, but she always came back so happy, he couldn't very well discourage her. Instead, he made it a habit to be there to help her gather them up. It was cute, seeing how she never just scooped them up and tucked them into the box. She always cradled them for a moment, rubbed them against her pleasure-flushed cheek, and temporarily lost all of her sadness. Usually she'd put them back, but it was barely eleven o'clock, and the day had turned into a scorcher. He'd promised to take care of her little chicks if she'd go in and cut a few checks he vowed were urgently needed.

Dylan watched the Nielson's Furniture truck drive up and nonchalantly wandered over to get a gander. It was time he could ill-afford to waste. "That the stuff for the baby?"

"Yep." Jim Nielson jumped out of the delivery truck. "This is the biggest order we've gotten in a long time."

Dylan let out a low whistle when the kid opened the

tailgate of the truck. "Need a hand getting all of this inside?"

"I'd be obliged. Dad promised her I'd set up everything. I may well still be in there clutching a screwdriver the day the kid comes home from the hospital!"

Dylan's smile faded. In fact, he gritted his teeth. Sondra was young. Pretty, too. Vulnerable. Some moon-eyed puppy like this could wriggle his way right into her heart if he did a few favors and acted understanding. Dylan half stomped up to the doorstep and pounded. "Sondra! Truck's here with the baby furniture!"

She opened the door and smiled at him. She didn't look at the truck—she looked at him! His heart did a genuine two-step. She was one fine-looking woman. He grinned right back like some nitwitted fool.

"Terrific!" She stepped back as Jimmy brought up the first load of boxes.

Steering her over to the couch, Dylan ordered, "You sit here and put your feet up. Did you want the baby to have the room next to the master bedroom?"

"Please."

Soon as they'd hauled the boxes inside, Sondra sat on the edge of the twin bed in the nursery and opened a box containing the swing. Dylan appreciated that about her—she was a dig-in-and-get-things-done kind of woman. She didn't expect everyone to fuss over her. Her attitude about getting on with life showed wisdom and strength.

She jutted her chin toward the far wall. "If you'd please put the crib over there, I'd appreciate it. It gets morning sun, but the baby won't be by the curtain's cord." She chewed on her lip. "I'm not sure about where to put the changing table."

Jabbing his thumb at the opposite wall, Dylan said, "There. When you're changing him, and he sprouts a leak, the closet and curtains are both out of range."

Sondra blinked at him. "How did you know that?"

"Mom was a baby magnet. Folks knew she'd watch their

kids anytime, for any reason. If someone was sick or needed a break or wanted to go off on a romantic getaway, they knew Mom would gladly take on their kids. I've changed more diapers than you could ever count," Dylan admitted gruffly.

She laughed, then turned. "I'll bet you're thirsty, Jim. Can I get you some lemonade or soda?"

"Either would be nice, ma'am. Thanks."

Sondra went down the hall toward the kitchen. Dylan followed right behind her. When she opened the refrigerator, he reached and grabbed a soda. Dylan was careful not to touch her. Oh, he loomed as close as possible, but he didn't actually allow himself to make contact. He just might end up doing something stupid if he did. Like shaking her 'til her teeth rattled. *Or kissing her.*

Yeah, he wanted to spin her around and plant a kiss on her. He ached to hold her and stop pretending to be nothing more than a helpful neighbor or financial partner. A man couldn't be more warped than this—to want a woman carrying another man's child. His timing stank. She didn't want him; he'd undoubtedly drive himself insane, wanting her.

He tried to concentrate on the soda. Sondra had asked what brand he preferred and kept some on hand for him. He'd been flattered. Now that the soda was waiting, ice cold, for him, he should have felt even better—but he didn't. He noticed she'd offered Jim a drink. Not him. Just Jim. He purposefully didn't straighten back up. His fingers flexed around the aluminum can as the cool air blasted out of the refrigerator.

"Please, Dylan, excuse me."

Something in her tone struck him as wrong. Mostly the way those last two words came out in a strained puff of air. He stepped back and wondered why she didn't uncurl. "Sondra?"

A long second passed. "Hmm?" Slowly, she straightened.

Scowling, he demanded, "What's going on?"

"Nothing."

"Baloney. You just shut the fridge and didn't get Jimmy-boy's drink."

Color tinged her cheeks. "Oh. I didn't, did I?" She opened the door again.

He slammed it shut. "Enough of this nonsense, woman. What just happened?"

"I had a little cramp, is all."

His can was on the countertop in nothing flat. Dylan scooped her up and headed for the couch. "It's too soon! Why didn't you say something straight off?"

eleven

Clutching his shoulders, she squeezed to stop his tirade. "Dylan, they're normal. The doctor calls them Braxton Hicks contractions. I can have four an hour without getting worried. It's simply a warm-up for the big event."

Stopping in the middle of the living room, he demanded, "Are you sure?"

"Yes."

His heart still thundered. "Just how many of those cramps have you been having?"

"Not that many."

He glanced at her belly. "Carrying a baby is normal, but you don't have to take it lightly. Cramps matter. Shouldn't you be counting them? We'll get a clock in here so you can keep track."

Her hand stayed stationary on his shoulder, but her thumb-nail traced back and forth along the seam of his shirt. A bashful half smile flickered across her face. "Honest, Dylan, I'm doing fine. I just saw the doctor day before yesterday."

"What did he say?"

"I'm fine." She cast a look back toward the kitchen and gave his shoulder a pat. "Your cola's getting hot."

"Do you care?"

Her eyes widened and mouth fell open. "Why else do you think I keep it in the refrigerator?"

He slowly bent and put her feet back on the floor. As he completely turned loose of her, he let out a rude snort.

"What is that supposed to mean?"

"You asked Junior what he wanted." He knew he sounded like a jealous kid who got the skimpiest slice of cake. "Just forget it."

Her small hands both grabbed and clasped one of his. "Dylan, I knew what you'd want. I don't know Jim Nielson from Adam, so I was trying to be polite."

"Oh." He yanked away his hand and growled, "Great. You think you know me so well that you can read my mind? For your information, I wanted lemonade!"

She planted her hands in the region where her hips used to be. "And I suppose that's why you took out a soda?"

"Do you want to stand here all day jawing, or do you want that crib put together?"

She sidled past him. "I'll get your lemonade."

He captured her wrist. "I don't expect you to wait on me. I can get my own drink."

"You've never treated me like I'm a waitress, Dylan. I appreciate all you do, and you're going the extra mile—again, helping with this on top of everything else. I—"

Whatever she was going to say got lost in a thump and a yelp from the other room. Dylan muttered, "I'd better get back in there with Jimmy-boy before he kills himself."

Sondra supplied the men with lemonade and fixed chicken salad sandwiches for lunch. They all sat in the nursery and admired the way things began to take shape. After wolfing down one last bite, Jim dusted his hands. "I gotta go. I took the liberty of tucking the high chair in the far side of the closet. You won't need it for a long while. Those blankets in there are a real kick."

Sondra opened the door, took out a big stack, and set them on the dresser. "Did I show these to you, Dylan?"

He picked up one. She'd carefully cut Kenny's flannel shirts into neat squares, stitched them together, and made baby quilts. "Wanna put this in the crib now?"

"Please."

As Sondra walked Jimmy out, Dylan put the other blankets away. A teddy bear tumbled out. Dylan stooped to pick it up. It was dressed in a tiny flannel shirt. Suddenly, Dylan felt completely out of place. He'd invaded her private domain. Just about the time he was feeling like his soda cans filled her fridge and he had a place in her home and life, he ran into the blatant reminder that in her heart, she still belonged to another man and was carrying his baby. Reality hit hard. He hurriedly stuffed the bear in place and strode to the front door. "I've got work to do. You rest up now."

"I don't do anything else." She paused, then said, "Dylan, I'm glad you were here to help me with the nursery. It made it easier. . . ."

He looked at her with a new tenderness. She gave her son special homemade blankets from a daddy he'd never know. Still, she appreciated Dylan's presence. That counted for a lot in his book. Unable to resist, he gently stroked his fingertips down her cheek. "Honey, you're gonna be a good mama."

"Thanks. Let me fix supper for you tomorrow night."

"You don't need to do that."

"I want to. I'm getting cabin fever, staying inside with nothing but the hum of the air conditioner. What would you like to have?"

"You have a knack in the kitchen. Do whatever sounds good to you." He worked like mad for the rest of the day to make up for the time he'd lost assembling the baby furniture.

The next day, Dylan got up early and pushed himself to get everything done. Teresa had given him a speculative look when he'd told her he already had plans and wouldn't be home for supper.

At ten 'til six, he shambled up to the back door and knocked. Sondra answered, looking fresh as a dewed wildflower. "Little lady, I'm as big a mess as a man ever was. I don't want to offend you, and I know you probably spent a lot of time fixin' a mighty fine meal, but I'll have to ask for a rain check."

Her gaze slid up and down him, then concentrated on his left sleeve. Her dainty nose twitched. That particular smell was unmistakable. "You have a change of clothes here. Hop on in and take a shower."

"I don't think—"

She grabbed his other arm and gave it a tug. "The cool air is rushing out while you stand there trying to act as if I don't know what manure smells like. Last time I checked, this was a ranch. It isn't as if it's a totally foreign part of the package." She shoved him in the direction of the hall, then flooded the kitchen with a mouthwatering aroma as she opened the oven to check on the rolls.

"Mmm. I won't be long."

A red-and-white-checkered cloth graced the table when he padded into the kitchen in his stocking feet. Her smile suddenly melted.

"What's wrong?"

She wiggled a little and blushed. "I can't. . .seem to. . .untie. . . oh! The apron strings are knotted."

"Come here." Dylan leaned against the counter and twirled her around. He deftly undid the small tangle. "What makes you wear an apron, anyhow? I thought those went out in the early sixties. Only time Teresa ever wears one is when she's basting half a cow for barbecue 'cause it's so messy."

"I drop everything down the front of me these days. I'm a first-class slob." She turned back around and let out a self-conscious laugh. "I guess I won't have any room to complain when the baby spills stuff all over his bibs and overalls."

"I've yet to hear you complain. Seems to me you've got cause to grouse a bit here and there."

For a minute, she couldn't seem to breathe. She closed her eyes. "I had to have the jeweler cut off my wedding band today."

"Aww." He pulled her into the shelter of his height as she steadied herself with a few deep breaths. "That's a pure pity. Why don't we get you a little something to wear so your finger doesn't feel so bare?"

"Nothing but Kenny's ring would feel right." She pushed away and forced a smile.

Dylan pulled her into his chest again and cupped her head to his shoulder. "How long has it been, sweetheart?"

"Seven months and three days."

She hadn't even had to think for a second before answering. He felt the waves of grief wash over her. He held her tightly, having to bow himself around her tummy. As if her grief wasn't enough, the baby kicked and squirmed between them— an ever-present and poignant reminder of a past she'd never leave behind. His lips barely grazed her temple as he quietly asked, "Want me to slip out of here?"

"No. Please, no!" Her fingers curled into the fabric of his chambray shirt. After taking another breath, she pushed away from him. "Supper's going to get cold. I hope you like Italian."

"The only thing I don't like is brussels sprouts. Other than that, I'm a human vacuum cleaner." He grinned at her and felt a flood of relief. The look of gratitude on her face made it clear he'd reacted the right way.

"Then you're in luck. In my opinion, they rate right up there with liver."

Wincing theatrically, Dylan held up both hands, as if to ward her off. "I know better than to touch that one!"

She'd made a marvelous meal. Manicotti, garlic bread, Caesar salad, and mixed vegetables should have been enough, but she even produced spumoni ice cream for dessert. "It's not chocolate, but I couldn't resist."

"You still could stand to put on a few pounds. I'm glad you didn't resist."

"Dylan, my weight isn't a topic of conversation."

"Then what about baby names? Are you going to name him after his dad?"

"Kenneth hated his name, so he made it clear from the get-go that he didn't want our son to be a Kenny, Junior. I thought about naming him after Miller, but it's cruel to stick a kid with a name like that. Imagine going through life with the name Thankful, Miller on the classroom rosters."

Tearing off a chunk of garlic bread, Dylan agreed, "That's bad."

"I thought maybe I'd look in the big, old family Bible Miller had in the study. There are probably a couple of good names in it."

"I'll clear the table, Sondra. Go get it and let's see what's to be found." Dylan rose and grabbed a few dishes. Sondra took a few steps and suddenly skidded. All of the plates in his hands clattered to the floor as Dylan made a quick dive. Miraculously, he caught her before she landed. "Oh!" she gasped as she grabbed handfuls of his shirt.

"Are you all right?" He didn't like how pale she'd become. Quickly scooping her into his arms, Dylan carried her to the living room and laid her on the couch. "Sondra, honey, are you hurt?"

Her hands went to her tummy. His joined them. Four hands, two slender and white, the others larger, rough, and tanned, waited impatiently until the child somersaulted. Sondra burst into nervous laughter.

Dylan sat on the floor. He wanted to hold her. At least hold her hand. He settled for reaching up and gripping the back of the couch to keep her in the shelter of his arm, but she started to squirm. *She doesn't want me close.*

"Dylan? I need to turn onto my side. It's hard to breathe if I'm on my back."

"Here." He slipped her arm around his neck and took his sweet time helping her get readjusted. The baby tumbled again, rippling across his wide-open palm in a startling display of strength. "He's a mighty little cowhand, isn't he?"

She let out another small, tight laugh and nodded.

Tilting her face upward, Dylan demanded, "How 'bout you, sugar? Are you all right after that spill?"

She nodded and proceeded to huddle into him and start to shudder.

"Shaken up," he evaluated. He couldn't blame her at all. His hands were unsteady. After a long time, her shivers tapered off. She mumbled an apology.

"You're gonna be all right, little Sondra. You and that baby are just fine."

"Just fine," she agreed.

"That's right, honey." The swell of emotions he felt stunned him. Tenderness the likes of which he'd never known filled his heart. It wasn't pity, either. It was a deep kind of caring. Oh, he felt attracted in a purely masculine sense. She was feminine and soft and yielding. Even now, pregnant as could be, the way she moved mesmerized him. He grazed her temple with his fingertips.

She smiled. "Not a single bump, in case you're checking. Your reflexes are awesome. Thanks for the rescue."

Her gorgeous, fiery locks splayed across the throw pillow. He wanted to toy with them, but that wouldn't do. Dylan pushed to his feet. "You stay put."

"Why? I'm—"

"Going to drive me nuts," he interrupted. He strode to the kitchen and made sure to clean up the small spot of spaghetti sauce she'd slipped in. She shouldn't be living alone anymore. It was dangerous. What if she'd fallen and been all by herself?

He heard a sound and went back to the living room, but it was empty. "Sondra?"

Her voice drifted to him from the hallway. "Just a minute."

"Are you okay?"

She reappeared. "Sorry I was so clumsy."

"You oughtn't be all on your lonesome. Teresa can come stay a little while, or—"

"No!" She stepped back. "I'm not a child. It's humiliating enough to have to rely on everyone to do my work around here. I refuse to have someone lurking around the house, watching my every move."

"What's wrong with letting us help you out a bit?"

"I'm going to work up to the day I have this baby. There's

no reason not to—I feel terrific. Besides, after I have him, I'll be out of commission for a couple of weeks."

"Six minimum. More likely, eight or ten."

"Ten!"

"If you have a caesarian."

"I'm not having a caesarian!"

Noting how she glowered at him and still managed to protectively cover the undercurve of her tummy, Dylan knew he'd rattled her. "Sondra, even if you don't, the baby is going to need you nonstop."

"I'll carry him in one of those nifty slings, so he'll go wherever I go."

"Your back aches from carrying him on the inside. What makes you think carrying him on the outside will be any easier?"

"Who says my back hurts?"

He gave her an exasperated look. "You're rubbing it right now. Fact is, most anytime I see you, you've taken to bracing the small of your back with your hands."

"See? I told you I need some privacy!"

"Tough luck. If you won't let someone stay with you, then we're going to start checking in on you a couple of times a day."

"That's ridiculous. Heaven help me—"

Dylan cracked a laugh. "If you're referring to Miller looking down at you from heaven, you'd better start worrying."

"I meant the Lord, Dylan. Still, it's sweet to think Miller is walking the streets of gold with God, and they can see how grateful I am."

"God's certainly watching over you, but I aim to help. As for Miller—I have news for you, Mother Hen: He was allergic to feathers. He put in that coop after he read your request for chicks."

"He never let on—"

He squeezed her arms. "Of course he didn't. That wasn't

Miller's way. When I asked him about it, he told me he got so much joy out of your visits and stories about the children, he'd have gladly built a coop ten times that size."

"He was a special man. I really miss him, Dylan."

He gave her hand a squeeze. "So do I."

"Thanks for coming over. I'm sorry I spoiled the evening."

"Hey, supper tasted terrific. You didn't spoil anything."

"I was clumsy as a cow."

Dylan forced himself to let go of her hand. He injected a mock sternness into his tone. "And here I thought you showed all of the potential to become a good rancher. Every cattleman knows cows are graceful as can be."

She turned him around and pushed him toward the front door. "And every cattlewoman knows cowboys are full of beans."

twelve

August arrived. Heat shimmered off of the land. Chores not done early in the morning became almost impossible to accomplish until late afternoon because of the torturous conditions. Sondra was eternally grateful for the air-conditioning in her home. It took less than five minutes in the noonday sun for her to wilt.

A philanthropic organization operated a summer camp for foster kids, so she didn't visit the group home. She missed seeing the kids, but she decided to concentrate on getting ready for the baby. She put sheets on the crib, wallpapered the nursery, and read voluminously.

Teresa offered to come help with the housework before and after the baby was born. Sondra appreciated her kindness but didn't accept. "I'll be bored to tears if I don't have anything to do. By then, you'll be a newlywed and need to settle in."

Teresa shook her finger. "Don't you be too proud to go changing your mind."

"I'm okay. Really, I am. Housework keeps me busy. At least I'll be ready when the baby decides to make his appearance."

"Once you drop, you shouldn't ought to be alone."

"You're as bad as Dylan! He's hovering. I'm just pregnant, not terminally ill."

"True enough. Still, if your water breaks, you'll need someone to drive you into the hospital lickety-split."

"I'm perfectly capable of driving myself."

Teresa gave her an appalled look. "You're not thinking clearly at all! Either you promise you'll call for help, or one of us is moving in with the other."

Dylan had come into the kitchen as her pronouncement

88

was made. He sauntered over to the refrigerator, pulled out a can of soda, and popped the lid. "Guess you have things under control. Which way is the move going? Sondra to our place, or you comin' here?"

"Neither!" Sondra glowered at him. "The last thing I need is having everybody drive me crazy. It's natural to have a baby. Healthy. If you don't want to believe me, I have books by all sorts of experts—"

He raised his can in a toasting gesture. "Hats off to you. You've done the schoolteacher thing and read a heap and did a bunch of research to get ready. Just remember that there's a world of difference between all of the theory in your ivory tower books and actual practice in real life situations."

"I've also gotten videos!"

He nearly choked on his soda, then shook his head. "Now why would a city-gal want to go do a thing like that?"

"City or country—what's the difference?"

"If you'd grown up out here, you would've seen animals give birth hundreds of times and figured it was. . .well, natural. I'll bet you've never even seen puppies born."

She lifted her chin. "I was there when you pulled that calf!"

Dylan winced at the memory. "If I'd have known you were expecting, I would've hustled you out of the birthing shed faster than a cricket can jump. Some things, you just don't have to watch—like those videos. Are you trying to scare yourself half to death?"

"The women in the movies all manage just fine."

He stared at her in silence. Suddenly, his face softened, as did his voice. His eyes glowed with compassion. "Yeah, Sondra, I'm sure they did, but they all had a husband along to smooth things out and help them along. You haven't wanted or asked for any help. No one expects you to hang in there and take it all by yourself. No one's going to bat an eye when you have 'em give you a little something to take the edge off of the pain."

"The American Academy of Pediatrics says that if drugs are used in labor, the choice should be based on what has the least effect on the neonate."

Dylan grinned. "See? The least effect."

Sondra looked at him in disbelief. "I've done tons of reading, and it still all boils down to the fact that the baby still gets some of the drug. That's why they say *if* drugs are used." She folded her arms across her chest and leaned back against the counter. She nodded resolutely. "I'm not about to subject my baby to any risk!"

"It seems to me you're putting him at risk by refusing to let anyone help you or stay with you." Dylan crushed the can in his hand, then tossed it into the trash. "If something went wrong, it might be too late by the time any of us got here."

"What an awful thing to say!"

"Yes, it was," Teresa agreed softly. She then tacked on, "It takes a mighty good friend to point out something that touchy, though. Dylan did it because he cares about you and the baby. You can't fault him for being dead straight honest."

"Excuse me." Sondra waddled out of the room and firmly shut her bedroom door. She had too much to worry about already. She didn't want to have them feed her any more concerns. Didn't they know how lonely she felt? How inept and overwhelmed? Didn't they understand she'd come here so her child would be well provided for and so she could stay with him?

It hadn't been easy in the least. The last thing she needed was for them to point out the obscure possibilities for complications. She stood at the crib and smoothed the sheet. A few moments later, she heard the kitchen door shut. Teresa and Dylan's voices faded away. Letting out a shaky sigh, Sondra knew she was alone once again. She didn't know whether to be delighted or worried.

&a.

Dylan knew exactly how to feel: guilty. He'd up and scared

the poor little widow-woman all over again. Often, when she wasn't watching, he checked her over really carefully, and her eyes managed to take on a desolate, haunted look.

Preoccupied, he rode Pretty Boy under a tree and whacked off his Stetson on a low hanging branch. By noontime, Dylan had made a fair number of dumb blunders. Knowing full well he'd best go square matters away with Sondra or practically kill himself in an accident, he stopped at home and took out a half-gallon brick of rocky road. Just as Sondra kept his brand of soda at her place, he'd taken to storing her favorite flavors of ice cream at his.

She didn't answer his knock, and Dylan started feeling antsy. He tried again, then walked on in. Tracking through the empty kitchen, he discovered the living room, bedrooms, and bathrooms were empty. Vexed, he walked back through the kitchen just in time to see the door to the basement open. Sondra stepped out.

She was wearing a gigantic, baby blue tee shirt. Singing loudly, she didn't realize he was there until she shut the door and took another step into the kitchen. As soon as she spied him, she let out a high-pitched shriek.

Dylan reached out to take the laundry basket from her.

"I'm so embarrassed!" An evasive move accompanied her wail.

Dylan kept hold of the basket. "For cryin' out loud, Sondra. You're covered up."

"Will you get out of here?"

"Nope." He glanced at the contents of the basket. Calm-as-you-please, he plucked her pink, fluffy housecoat from the top of the laundry, shook it out, and slipped it around her shoulders. Curling his hands around the basket, he ordered, "Give this to me."

"Only if you promise to close your eyes and turn around."

Huffing, he complied. "Okay." He stood with his back to her, set the basket on the table, and decided to lessen the tension. "Remember those fluffy, round, pink lunch cakes?"

"Are you comparing me to one of those?"

"Yup. One of those pinky, dinky, sweet things."

She muttered, "As if there's anything dinky about me."

Dylan snagged the belt from the laundry basket. He turned around and proceeded to slip it around her, then tie it in a quick clove hitch. He patted the knot where it lay over the mound of her tummy and winked at her. "I defy you to look down and tell me you don't look just like—"

"Dylan?" she interrupted. "I'm not a violent woman, but I'm about to threaten grave, bodily harm if you don't hush."

"Didn't you ever learn about getting more flies with honey than vinegar? Instead of grousing, you should try to bribe me into silence by offering ice cream."

She gave him an exasperated look.

He held up his hands in a gesture of surrender. "I met you more than halfway—I brought the ice cream. Tell you what, you go sit on the sofa, and I'll bring you some."

She slipped past him and headed for the hallway, mumbling, "I don't want flies."

Dylan knew she hadn't gone to the living room, but he didn't chase after her. She was too embarrassed for him to push matters. He could hear her walking around in the master bedroom. If it made her feel better to pull on fifteen layers of clothes, he was going to let her—and he wouldn't say a word about it. After filling a pair of bowls, he went to the living room and ate several heaping bites while he waited.

Sondra reappeared wearing stretch slacks and a gauzy top the color of spring grass. She didn't meet his eyes when she finished easing herself into the corner of the couch.

Dylan pressed the bowl into her hands. "I changed my mind. The minute you turned your back and started walking down the hallway, I thought you looked like a polar bear with a sunburn."

"Well!" The affronted tone of voice was at direct odds

with the smile on her face. "I'm offended. You could have said I looked like something cool and graceful—like, say. . .a flamingo."

"Nah. I'm not gonna encourage a nitwit notion like that. You might well take it in your mind to stand on one leg. You've managed to do just about everything else imaginable, but some things defy good sense."

She played with the spoon and ice cream. "I've been careful. I admit—it's driving me crazy not to do more around here, though. Holding back goes against my grain."

Dylan set down his ice cream. "You do plenty. It's not easy, adjusting to a new home. You're settling in and making friends. Keeping books and learning the ropes of a new business, too. Using your mind is every bit as valuable as using your muscles."

She swirled her spoon around and concentrated on the bowl as if she'd never seen anything half as intriguing. Her nonchalance was feigned, and poorly, at that.

Dylan leaned forward. "I confess, when we started out, I figured this was as lopsided as a partnership ever got. You've pitched in, dug deep, and have surprised everyone—me, most of all." She looked up at him. Her gaze locked with his, as if she needed to be certain he wasn't just giving her a pep talk. Dylan stared back at her, steady and sure. He wanted her to know she'd earned his admiration.

"You've been terrific about setting aside your plans and throwing yourself into this partnership. My role has been negligible. You'll never know how thankful I am."

He acknowledged her words with a dip of his head. "Mrs. Thankful, I do believe your name suits you fine."

She hitched her shoulder. "Other than the baby, it's about all I have to claim of Kenny's."

She didn't often say much about her husband. He wondered aloud, "How long were you together?"

"We dated for about four months."

Dylan picked up his ice cream again. "But how long were you together?"

"I thought you knew. I um. . ." A virulent blush swept over her as her voice dropped shyly. "I got pregnant on our honeymoon. Kenny called it beginner's luck."

"But he died—" Dylan rasped, "You were married only two months?"

Her eyes filled with tears. "Six weeks and two days."

"Aww, baby." Dylan reached to pull her close.

She shoved her bowl into his hands instead. "I can't even eat that for solace!"

"Why not?"

A wry smile twisted her lips, even as her eyes swam with tears. "Because the baby has the hiccups!"

Dylan thumped the bowls down on the coffee table. "Really?"

She let out a watery laugh. "Look—you can see it."

His gaze locked on her tummy, and within a few seconds, his hands were there, too. Rhythmic knocking lifted and dropped her belly. Soon, he couldn't feel it because her laughter made everything shake. "You ought to see the look on your face, Dylan!"

"That's wild!"

"It's rude. I'll have to teach this kid manners as soon as he makes an appearance."

"Don't ask me for any help. I'm the idiot who barged in on you today. I'm real sorry for that, you know."

Sondra patted his arm. The distraction of the baby's hiccups seemed to have bought her an opportunity to regain control of her emotions. "It was my fault. I invited you to come and go at will. The dress I wanted to wear today is down in the dryer. I just dashed down to get it, but it was still too damp to wear." She started to wallow.

"What are you doing?"

"I'm trying. . .to. . .get up!"

Dylan sprang to his feet. "Why didn't you just ask for help?"

"I'm. . .not. . .helpless." She let him haul her to her feet and excused herself.

Dylan knew she was heading for the bathroom. "I'll see you later. Oh—Sondra?"

She stopped.

"Teresa asked me to have you give her a call. Something about the wedding."

She gave him a winsome smile. "Okay." She watched his expression change. "What is it?"

"Something you said just passed through my mind."

"What?"

"You said it was a honeymoon baby."

"Yes."

Beginner's luck. She and Ken waited, just as God commands.

Sondra turned and started down the hallway. She called over her shoulder, "Thanks for the ice cream."

Dylan took his empty bowl and her melted mush into the kitchen. Rinsing them, he shook his head in utter astonishment. She'd had a single spoonful of ice cream, just as she'd had a single month of passion. However sweet a month of honeymooning had been, it couldn't make up for a lifetime of loneliness or the responsibilities of bearing and rearing a child. No wonder Sondra still clung to Kenny's shirts and wanted to save the rip in the sofa. She had hardly any memories and nothing else at all.

thirteen

Three days later, Dylan rapped on the back door. Sondra opened it, and he entered quickly so the hot air wouldn't rush in and heat up the house. "Need a drink?"

"Probably."

"Help yourself." She turned to leave the kitchen.

Dylan gently grabbed hold of what once had been her waist. "Hang on. Every time I get within ten yards of you, you drop out of sight like a prairie dog diving into the nearest hole. Why are you avoiding me?"

Sondra didn't bother to deny his assertion.

Dylan murmured, "You're still not looking me in the eye. Are you having a fit because I saw you in that big tee shirt, or are you embarrassed that I ferreted out that you were a virgin bride?"

Her cheeks tingled with heat. "I'm not ashamed of having waited for marriage."

"So you're being goosey because I saw you looking like one of the seven dwarfs?"

"Is that what you thought?"

"I think I'm ready for that drink now." He opened the refrigerator, got out a soda for himself, and handed her the milk. He gave her a wink and added, "You're getting a tad moody. Isn't that supposed to mean you're ready to have the little one?"

"Don't we just wish!"

"September second is eighteen days away. I counted on the calendar this morning."

"In eighteen days, I'm going to take out a full page ad in the county newspaper, offering my services as a crop dusting dirigible!"

His soda went down the wrong way, and he spluttered.

Sondra whacked him on the back a few times, then simpered, "Mr. Ward, I do believe that served you right after calling me moody."

"If the shoe fits. . ."

She made a face at him and grudgingly admitted, "I am grumpy today."

"So I see. Why?"

Heat and color flooded her face. "Never mind."

"Hmmm. Must be something terrible. Something like stretch marks."

"I don't have those!" As soon as she reacted, she groaned and turned away.

"I'm not trying to offend you. I'm trying to help and listen. You're not making this easy at all!"

"Shouting at me doesn't make it any easier," she yelled back. "You can't possibly understand how humiliating it is to get so fat you can't fit behind the wheel!" As soon as the admission was made, she let out a shriek.

Dylan blocked her exit. "Where did you want to go?"

"Away from you!"

A grin twitched at the left corner of his lips. "I meant, where did you want to drive?"

She bowed her head and mumbled, "I had a doctor's appointment."

"Does it occur to you that if I have time to stop for a drink, I could take you?"

"Ten minutes for a soda is far different that an hour drive in each direction and the time in between at the office."

"Bravo. You can do math. I'll take you today. Nickels, Howie, or Teresa can take you next week. After that, there's no problem, because Junior will make his appearance."

"I don't need to go today."

His brow puckered. "You just said you had an appointment."

"It was at nine o'clock. I cancelled it."

"What?! That was the stupidest thing I've ever heard!"

She glowered at him. "If you think I enjoy having to depend on everyone around here, you can just guess again! I refuse to ask anyone to do anything more for me."

Dylan slammed his can down and bellowed, "Then you've got your priorities wrong, lady. Let the dumb ranch fall apart at the seams for all we care! Just take care of the poor baby!" He spun around, stomped out of the house, and slammed the door shut.

&

September second came and went. Sondra still hadn't had the baby. Her nerves were frayed, and she'd spent the last twenty days studiously avoiding Dylan Ward. She managed to be in the bathroom, on the phone, or somehow unavailable whenever he made an appearance. Church was the only place she couldn't avoid him, but he kept busy as an usher so she didn't have to do more than merely greet him with a polite nod.

Half of the time, she was livid that Dylan dared to think she'd ever put anything above her baby's welfare. The other half of the time, she was embarrassed she'd given him so much latitude in her life that he felt free to speak to her that way.

If only he hadn't been such a good listener, so calm and undemanding, so kind and helpful. If only he hadn't let her weep on his shoulder and gently gotten her through her illness. . .maybe then she would have kept a sense of perspective. But she hadn't. She'd opened her big mouth and spilled every intimate detail of her whole life. His rock-solid presence, understated ways, and quiet attentiveness all made it easy to keep company with him—but she could resist those qualities if she made a conscious effort. The truth of it was, he'd found her Achilles' heel. She found it impossible to resist a man who loved God and rocky road.

Dylan still saw to all of the ranching matters, and he'd taken to phoning her to transmit any information regarding bills or expenditures. She managed to be businesslike and polite, but an awkward distance stretched between them.

That distance left her feeling bereft. In many ways, it also made her feel crushingly guilty. Though she grieved for Kenny, she still thought of Dylan. He crossed her mind way too much, as a matter of fact. He'd somehow managed to fill in places in her life and heart that went far, far beyond a simple business partner's role.

She'd been stupid to let that happen. Now that it had, part of her wanted to shut down that connection; worse, part of her secretly wanted to tend the relationship and let it not only continue, but deepen. What kind of widow leaned on a man when she'd lost her husband so recently and was pregnant with his child? Confused, lonely, and guilty, she kept to herself.

Sitting at the kitchen table, Sondra stared at a bowl of ice cream. She missed Dylan's impish smile, the rumble of his deep voice, the companionship they'd shared. She didn't understand the emptiness she felt. Twice during her courtship and once during their marriage, Kenny had to take a week-long business trip. She'd missed him, but not like this. This odd ache took her by surprise. How had Dylan wormed his way into her life like this?

❧

Dylan took a long, tepid drink from the garden hose. He'd far rather have a tall glass of sweet tea, but the welcome he'd once felt in Sondra's house was long gone. The contact he'd had with her had been the highlight of each day—a short interlude of laughter, planning, camaraderie, and mutual regard. That evaporated in this estrangement.

The distance between them puzzled him. He'd been blunt, but honest—and she'd taken it badly. As he cranked off the faucet, a last bit of water drained from the hose and made a puddle of mud. Yeah, he'd made muck of everything.

He'd had enough of this strain. Playing games never suited him. Saturday was Teresa's wedding, and if he didn't do something quick, Sondra would probably concoct a flimsy excuse and not show up, just to avoid him. He'd been biding his time, but she needed a nudge. She needed folks' friendships and support, Teresa's feelings would be hurt if Sondra didn't come, and. . .well, he missed her company.

"Nickels," he called across the barnyard, "I need a word with you." After he arranged for Nickels to drive Sondra to the wedding, he whistled as he strode off. Things were going to fall into place.

❧

The photographer snapped portraits out on the church lawn, but Dylan left and strode over to the car. After he helped Sondra out, he whistled under his breath. "Aren't you pretty as can be?"

Sondra glanced at the striped canopy in the near distance, then looked down at her apple green and white maternity dress in utter dismay. She didn't manage to stifle her moan. "I match the tent we're going to be dining under!"

"No wonder you look good enough to eat," he shot back with a wink. He tucked her into a pew in the air-conditioned sanctuary, then rejoined the wedding party.

Sondra sat through the whole ceremony remembering her own wedding. It, too, had been small. Kenny had worn a white tux just like Jeff's. Some days, it was so hard to pretend that she was getting along well. This was one of them, yet she plastered a smile on her face. Teresa bent over backward to be a good friend. She deserved to have everyone celebrate her joy—not grow selfishly maudlin.

An intimate wedding, the bridal party consisted only of Teresa, Jeff, the matron of honor, and the best man. Dylan served as the best man, and Sondra couldn't help noticing how handsome he looked. He'd been kind to come walk her into the church. Had he sensed how hard today would be for her?

Sondra planned to sit toward the edge of the reception tent so she could duck away. To her amazement, Teresa tugged her to the bride's supper table. Dylan was her partner, and the matron of honor's husband partnered her. The whole arrangement felt horribly awkward.

The conversation stayed lively, thanks to Teresa's bubbly nature and Jeff's crazy sense of humor. Dylan glanced around and signaled the waiter with a suave motion. The waiter scuttled over, and Dylan quietly stated, "The lady and I would like sparkling cider in our toasting glasses."

Sondra slanted him a look. "You know I don't drink. Why are you playing Pregnancy Police?"

He simply chortled.

Jeff leaned forward. "What was so funny? What did I miss?"

"I told the waiter to get us sparkling cider so I could do the toast," Dylan tattled. "She's accusing me of being part of the Pregnancy Police."

Bride and groom both laughed; then Teresa smiled. "You've got a whole squadron of us."

Not wanting to put a damper on things, Sondra accepted the new glass, then tilted it at Teresa. "Just you wait. One of these days, your turn is coming."

"I hope so!" She blushed.

"Yeah, me, too." Jeff waggled his brows.

Dylan stood and gave a witty, surprisingly sentimental toast. He was quite a man—more masculine than Adam on the day of creation, capable of running two ranches, and still tenderhearted toward his sister. . .*and good to me*.

That admission made the defenses Sondra tried to put up crumble. She'd been a fool to try to shut him out of her life. He'd let her withdraw, but he hadn't neglected his duties. Now he was including her as if nothing was wrong. . .*and it isn't*, a little voice whispered in her heart. Nothing was wrong. Dylan still cared for her.

"Sondra?" He cupped her elbow and gave the glass in her hand a puzzled look. She'd taken a sip, but everyone else started talking while she stood frozen in place. "Are you okay?"

She barely kept from scooting closer to him. As she set her

glass down on the white linen tabletop, she whispered, "The heat must be getting to me."

"I'll take you home."

"No!" The last thing she wanted was for him to give up the only day he'd taken off for pure enjoyment since she'd taken possession of the Curly Q. Needing to signal their friendship was back on track, she stammered, "I'll have a seat and drink more cider. It's just that I need to leave before they cut the cake."

He pulled a bit closer. "Why?"

She waited a beat then started to laugh. "Remember what happens when you and I get near desserts?"

❧

Dylan sat in his kitchen and dialed Sondra's number, but the line buzzed. *Busy. It's probably for the best. She gets under my skin too easily. I need to pay more attention to the ranches. One is more than enough to keep a man busy; two is far too much.*

He, Teresa, and Jeff had come to an agreement about leaving the Laughingstock Ranch undivided and splitting profits for the time being. With his livestock and Sondra's mingling in the pastures, it would be a disaster to take down or move fences at this point. Jeff and Teresa adamantly stated that the land and livestock he gained from Miller's bequest at the end of the year were Dylan's alone. They didn't expect a share of that windfall.

Dylan did a bit of figuring and estimated what the size of his herd would be once the dust settled. It would take a few years to build up his stock once Jeff and Teresa's half moved onto Langston property, but in the meantime, he'd grow less fodder—or continue production and sell the excess. He'd have to give some thought to letting the land lie fallow.

One thing for certain, land could be left unproductive for a season, but busy little Sondra probably wouldn't let grass grow under her feet. Silly woman didn't know the value of a field left unseeded or a moment left to leisure. He shook his head.

How did his brain twist that direction?

She'd looked sweet as could be at the wedding—but she'd wilted all too fast at the reception. For the first time, she'd admitted she might be slowing down a bit. She valued her independence and got downright feisty whenever she figured anyone was trying to bulldoze her.

Self-reliance rated as a fine quality, and he respected the gutsy woman for charging ahead with life. She didn't wring her hands or bemoan her calamities; she took a deep breath and kept plowing ahead. Too bad she didn't understand that could be dangerous at times. She needed someone to temper her autonomy and moderate her drive. Sondra could easily misjudge her ability and get hurt—and that wasn't even taking into consideration her motherly condition. Heaven only knew how often he prayed for her safety and health. Yes, knowing Sondra certainly improved his prayer life.

She must be going stark raving mad, not having had the baby yet. What if she slipped in the kitchen or shower? And those stairs to the basement were steep. He didn't want to think about her carrying a laundry basket up and down them. No matter what image came to mind, each task was fraught with danger.

He tried to stay calm, but Dylan wanted to grab the phone and announce that he was moving in until the baby came. No, make it for a period including the first few weeks afterward when Sondra would need extra help. Miller asked him to look after her. He was the logical choice. After all, Teresa needed to take care of her own home and husband. None of the hands knew a thing about babies. Yes, Dylan knew he was the best man for the job. . .but Sondra wanted him in her home just about as much as she wanted whooping cough.

He could probably work around that. The clincher was the morality issue. Plenty of men and women shacked up without the benefit of marriage, but Dylan didn't approve. It went against his personal code to give anyone the slightest reason to question the morality of his actions. It made for a poor witness and opened a Christian to temptation. A man and a woman ought not live together without the benefit of marriage—well, unless some extreme situation dictated otherwise.

Try as he might, he couldn't stretch the facts that far. Sondra was one fine-looking woman. If he moved in, folks might well cook up some suspicions and gossip. *What kind of witness would that be?* A thought occurred to him. He picked up the phone and dialed. This time, it rang. And rang. And rang. By the fifth ring, he was ready to call paramedics to meet him at her place, but a breathless voice answered, "Hello?"

"Sondra? Are you all right?"

A short, mirthless laugh met his inquiry.

"What's so funny?"

"Absolutely nothing."

"Then why are you laughing?"

"Because I promised myself that if anyone else called me and asked if I'd had the baby yet, I'd do something rash."

"Oh." He paused, then said in a level tone, "I guess it's a good thing I didn't ask."

"So what do you need?"

"Is Kenny's family coming to help you when the baby's born?"

"No!"

Dylan jerked at how harsh she sounded. "It was just a thought."

"They want nothing to do with the baby."

"What!"

"You heard me. I'm tired, Dylan. Did you need anything else?"

"It may not be my business, but an explanation would be nice."

She sighed. "It's a long story."

She'd said she was tired, but in an instant, she'd gone from sparky to sad, and he didn't want to hang up without making sure she was okay. He'd hit a nerve, and it bothered him. He quietly invited, "Give me the Reader's Digest condensed version."

A long silence crackled over the line. Sondra sighed. "The Thankfuls equated Kenny's injury with complete disability. His parents presumed he wasn't capable of. . .being a complete husband. They want nothing to do with a baby they're sure isn't their son's, and they threatened to cut their daughter off without any college funds if she kept in contact with me."

"Oh, Sondra!" Dylan breathed in shocked sympathy.

"It doesn't matter. My son and I will get along just fine without them."

"Sure, you will." *Comfort. How can I comfort her, Lord? Help me take away the sting of their rejection.* His gaze happened to land on the refrigerator, and inspiration struck. "I'm dying for some ice cream. What if I grab a carton and come over?"

"Sorry. I'm lousy company. I'm just going to go to bed."

"Okay. Sweet dreams, honey."

❧

Sondra hung up the phone, sat down, and cried. The weatherman took unholy glee in announcing the temperature hit all-time records for the fourth day in a row. She bet he wouldn't be half that perky if his wife were overdue and suffering from the heat.

Her attitude disintegrated even further over the next week. Twelve days overdue, she strained to be barely civil.

"Mornin', city-gal," a soft, teasing drawl sounded from beside her as she sat on the porch steps just past sunrise the next day.

Sondra jumped. "How'd you get here without me knowing it?"

Dylan gave her a lazy grin. "Because you're not all here, if you get my drift."

"If I were any more 'here,' my feet would grow roots."

"Ah. . .cabin fever. A terrible case of it, if I don't miss my guess." Dylan took a seat beside her, rested his forearms on his knees, and stared off at the horizon. "I need to tend to some things, but I'll come by tonight at seven. I'll take you to town, and we'll get an ice cream cone."

"I'm pathetic, aren't I?"

Dylan gave consideration to her question, then pursed his lips as he turned to study her. A scampish grin tilted his mouth, and his wink warned her he was about to deliver one of his tongue-in-cheek zingers. "I don't think I'd tag you as pathetic. More pitiful, if you ask me."

"Oh, get out of here!"

"Are you talking to me or the baby?"

❧

Dylan was going to have to hurry to be at Sondra's on time. A man had to be in sorry shape if all he could think about the whole livelong day was eating an ice cream cone with a pregnant widow. Dylan glanced at a mirror and saw the sorriest looking man he'd ever seen.

The phone rang, and he barked, "Hullo," as he clamped the receiver between his shoulder and ear so he'd have both hands free to yank on a sock.

"Dylan, there's been a change—"

"Oh, no, there hasn't," he interrupted. "You have to get out a bit. What harm is there in a trip to Dairy Queen?"

"I changed my mind. . .or maybe I should say my mind was changed."

"So change it back."

"Dylan, I don't want you to argue with me."

Stubborn woman. "Do you even know what you want?"

She went quiet for a moment, then said in a strained voice, "I want you to take me to the hospital."

fourteen

"The hospital!" He nearly dropped the phone and managed to jam his other sock painfully between his toes in his rattled state.

"Teresa's not home, and—"

"I'll be right over!"

"I think I'd better get moving. The contractions are getting strong—"

She went silent, and he barked, "You hang on. I'll be there in a jiffy." He hung up.

He didn't bother to button his shirt, drove like a maniac, and came to a screeching halt in front of her place.

Cool as a cucumber, she sauntered down the steps and opened the passenger door. "Thank you for coming."

He hopped out of the cab and hastily fastened his shirt as he went around to her side. In those brief seconds, she tucked a little suitcase into the cab. Her methodical actions didn't reassure him in the least. He'd learned when things were tough, Sondra got very subdued and businesslike. "How far apart are the contractions?"

She gave no answer. Instead, she started to pant softly. Her hand went to her tummy and brushed back and forth in cadence with her breathing. After a minute, she let out a sigh and gave him a wobbly grin. "I'm about as ready as I'm going to be."

"You were ready weeks ago." He grinned for her benefit. If she wanted to put an I'm-okay veneer over this, he'd play along. "You're fretting like a hen, 'bout ready to nest on her egg awhile. Guess we'd best get you to the hatchery—I mean, hospital."

Her lips bowed up in a smile. He knew he'd done the right thing. She needed him to be calm. *Yeah, that's me, all right. Mr. Easygoing. . . Relaxed as barbed wire and sedate as a charging bull. She'll never know, though. I'll play it mellow, act unruffled, and she'll stay composed.*

"Upsy-daisy." He gently cupped her middle and hoisted her into the truck, then pulled her seat belt out so it reached its fullest length. She snagged the buckle and snapped it into the holster. He'd have rather fastened it himself. It would have given him a good excuse to get close and kind of hug her. That realization made him mad at himself. He needed to get his head examined. He needed to get *her* examined.

She started panting once again.

"Just hang on!" He slammed her door shut, raced around, and vaulted into his seat. They were in motion before his door closed. He quickly buckled his seat belt and shot her a worried look. "How close together are the contractions?"

She didn't answer right away—a fact that made him antsy as could be. Finally, she let out a deep sigh and whispered, "Six minutes or so."

"Six min—"

"Dylan?" She squeezed his arm. He cut off his impending tirade and waited for whatever she wanted to say. She smiled sweetly as her cheeks filled with color. "Could we still stop by Dairy Queen and get me an ice cream cone to eat on the way?"

❧

It should have been an hour-long drive to the hospital; they made it in thirty-nine minutes. Traffic had been light, and though he normally drove in a conservative manner, Dylan turned into a maniac behind the wheel. Sondra gave him a couple of worried glances and muffled more than a few gasps at the harrowing way he drove.

Each time she gasped, he moaned, "Another one? Already?"

She wasn't sure whether to say anything or not. The man looked downright sick. He looked like he needed medical attention more than she did! In fact, he acted as rattled as she felt. If she had any sense of humor left, she would have thought it was pretty funny that she was hurting and he was sweating bullets, but she'd forgotten how to laugh, and a thousand fears and doubts assailed her.

For all of his panic, Dylan carried on with his trademark kindness. "Hang on, Sondra. I'll have you there real soon."

"I'm okay."

"Sure you are." His eyes accused her of lying, but he didn't challenge her. Instead, he wondered, "Why are you clutching that teddy bear so tight?"

"He's my focal point. I'm supposed to stare at him when I'm having a contraction."

"My staple gun's under the seat. Want me to stick him to the dash so you can relax a little?"

"What?!"

"Forget it. That was a bad idea. I just thought maybe you'd like your hands free to rub your belly."

"I have two hands."

Dylan chuckled softly. "Once the baby's here, you're going to wish you had another pair. He's going to keep you mighty busy."

"It'll be a nice change. I've been bored to tears for weeks now."

"Have you missed taking the little chicks to the kids?"

She nodded. "Nickels volunteered to do it for a while so I can get the baby settled."

"That'd be real fine," he said. He tried to carry on a bit of conversation to distract her. It didn't work, but she appreciated the effort—as long as he kept his staple gun out of sight.

Relief flooded her when she saw the hospital. "You can drop me off at—"

"Drop you off? Are you out of your mind?"

Sondra dug her fingers into the teddy's plush brown fur and began to pant once again. She'd done her best to keep from moaning, but the pains kept growing stronger. She didn't want Dylan to see her lose control. Having him think well of her mattered too much—more than she'd ever confess.

Early in life, she'd learned to keep some walls up to protect herself from being hurt. She'd let down the walls with Kenny—and now, look what that got her. A heart full of grief and waves of gut-wrenching pain.

Dylan was already too adept at slipping past her defenses. When she realized she'd started into labor, she'd longed to call him—to have him drop everything and be with her. Instead, she convinced herself to hold off, then call Teresa. When Teresa failed to answer, she'd felt a flare of gladness that she had an excuse to lean on Dylan yet again. Though heading for heartache, she couldn't seem to stop herself.

The next contraction hit. *Lord, help me through this. I need Your strength. I can't do this on my own.* She made it through and let out another cleansing breath. She hoped it didn't sound weak and choppy to Dylan.

He parked and came around to help her out. His long, ropy arm went across her in an almost-hug. He held it for a heartbeat before he unlatched her seat belt.

For an instant, Sondra nearly yielded to the temptation to lean into his warmth. *No. It's not right. He's a partner. Okay, he's a friend.* The temptation to depend on him was frightening. He'd made it so easy for her to rely on his wisdom and strength. There wasn't another soul on earth she'd ever counted on like this. Physically vulnerable and emotionally raw, she forced herself to lean back into the truck seat.

"Another one?"

She wet her lips and shook her head. Dylan must've figured she couldn't slide out without his support. He tempered his strength to pull her free, then set her on her feet. The movement triggered an unexpected contraction, and she cried out.

"It's all right, darlin'. Here—let me help you."

She'd knotted his shirt in her palms, but she shook her head. Her eyes swam with unshed tears and her voice sounded thick as she quavered, "I'll manage. I'll call you—"

"What kind of man do you think I am, Sondra? How could I possibly leave you when you need so much help?" He tilted her face up to his. His steady, somber eyes read the emotion on her face and he interpreted it aloud. "You've never had anyone to rely on. You're used to doing things for yourself."

She nodded.

"Not this time."

She ought to order him to go home. Deep in her heart, though, she wanted to throw her arms around him and hang on tight. Confusion and pain muddled her thinking.

"Here we go," he said softly as he slipped one arm around her and grabbed her suitcase with the other. "We'll make it through together."

❧

Two hours later she bit her lip, clenched her eyes shut, and gripped his wrist as the next pain hit. When it finally ended, Dylan straightened up.

Sondra grabbed for him. "No! I need *you!*"

Dylan went stock-still and looked down at her. No one had ever needed him. No one. Not once, ever. Oh, they'd needed his time, his knowledge, his strong back, a helping hand. . .but the truth was plain to see. Sondra needed *him*. All at once, something deep inside that had been so impossibly empty suddenly filled to overflowing.

The full truth finally hit him hard. He'd been praying for the right woman—here, now, he knew deep in his soul he'd finally found her. All along, he'd fought the truth, denying she was the one. He'd tried to chalk it up to feeling protective. To doing Miller a favor. Feeling sympathetic. Basic chemical attraction that clouded his thinking. He should have known. He'd been fighting the inevitable, but suddenly the last piece fell into place: She'd let him know the feelings weren't just one-sided.

The assurance nearly bowled him over, yet it filled him

with a joy that he'd never dared hope would be his. It didn't matter that she was having Kenny's son. Dylan would love him every bit as much as if he were his own. She needed him. This woman who always tried to face storms all by herself was clinging to him for dear life. She wanted him here, now. At the most vulnerable time in her life, he was there to help her through and share the miracle at the end. A man couldn't ask for more.

She shuddered with another pain and pled in a shaky voice, "Don't leave me."

He leaned close and promised, "I'm not going to leave you, Sondra." *Lord, please help her. She can't take much more.*

As rapidly as that panicky time started, it came to an abrupt halt. She curled forward, grabbed the rail, and gritted, "I've gotta push!"

The doctor had just come in. He finished snapping on a glove. "Let me check to see if it's time." A minute later, he ordered, "Hang on. Don't push. Blow."

Dylan looked from Sondra to the doctor. The doc grimaced as he finished the exam. He ordered over his shoulder, "Call anesthesiology."

Dylan's heart dropped to the toes of his boots. *Almighty Father, don't let anything go wrong.*

The doctor stripped off his glove and threw it away. He squeezed Sondra's arm. "We're going to have to do a caesarian."

Dylan grabbed Sondra's hand and held it tightly sandwiched between both of his. "Why?"

The doc shook his head. "Face presentation. The baby flexed his head so he's trying to come through face first. It's impossible. We'll have to section her."

❧

"Nine pounds even," Dylan marveled as he finished buckling Matthew into the car seat.

"Congratulations, ma'am," the volunteer said. "You, too, sir. He's the spitting image of you."

Pain twisted Sondra's heart. How many times in the last few days had someone presumed Dylan was the baby's father? It was an understandable mistake. . . . But every time it happened, intense longing struck. She wanted her husband. Matthew deserved a daddy. God provided Dylan as a temporary fill-in, but that wasn't the same thing.

Dylan murmured, "Come on, Sondra. Get in the car."

She awkwardly lowered herself into the backseat so she could sit next to her son. Dylan pressed a tissue into her hand, buckled her seat belt, then winked. "Aren't you just the cutest little mama in three counties? I swear, your tummy and ankles are just about back to normal already!"

"Who cares?" she wailed. He said nothing, but his eyes narrowed and mouth tightened. "I'm sorry!"

"Hush. You'll wake up PeeWee. You both ought to nap on the trip home." He took one of the flannel shirt blankets she'd made and draped it across her and the baby. "I'll run the air conditioner, so you'll probably want this as protection from the draft."

He remembered to bring Kenny's shirt blanket. I'm being a total shrew, and Dylan keeps being nice. Sondra choked out an apology, and he patted her hand. She tamped down her tears and leaned back against the upholstery. Within a few miles, her lids grew heavy. The next thing she knew, Matthew started crying. She peeled open her eyes and gently caressed the dark peach fuzz on his head. Dylan glanced back and smiled. "We'll be home in a jiffy."

"Dylan, thank you for all of the help. I don't know—"

"Don't go getting all flowery on me. What are friends for?"

"All I do is take. You've been on the giving end of this relationship since day one."

"Sharing the miracle of your son's birth was the most precious gift I've ever been given. You're plumb crazy if you think otherwise."

He stopped in front of her place and started to chuckle; she groaned. "Half of the world is here."

"Nah. Just the folks from your spread and mine. Teresa arranged it. Otherwise, all of these curious men are going to slip up to the house and bother you at inopportune moments."

Matthew's cries turned into full scale, outraged bellows. "Dylan, this *is* an inopportune moment!"

Teresa opened the door and crooned to the baby. "There, now. Don't you fret. It's lunchtime for everyone. Your mama will feed you while all of these big ol' cowboys chow down. They're dying to meet the littlest boss."

"Teresa, you carry in PeeWee; I'll take care of his mama." Dylan handed Matthew to his sister and smiled. "Careful. He's as loud as he is big!"

Sondra felt self-conscious about having Dylan haul her inside, but she wasn't sure she could manage to mount the steps under her own steam. He carried her easily and took her back to the master bedroom. "I'll bring in your suitcase. You'd best better slip into a nightie before you get too tired to manage on your own."

"Oh, no. I'm staying dressed!"

"Don't be knot-headed, Sondra."

Before she could argue anymore, Teresa interrupted, "This little fellow isn't going to wait much longer. Dylan, you get on outta here. Sondra, honey, if you don't change, Matthew isn't going to be able to get to the table, so to speak. That dress zips clear on up the back. Dylan's right. Put on a nightie, else these men'll think you're holding court and won't ever get back to work. Once they see your robe, they'll keep it short and sweet."

❧

"Short and sweet, just like you," Dylan teased a little while later as the last of the hands left, the door shut, and the house fell silent. "Told you so."

Sondra patted Matthew and let her head fall back onto the sofa cushion. "Those have to be the three ugliest words in the English language."

" 'Go to bed' has to rate close to the top on the list of the best phrases."

"Far be it from me to put up a fuss." Sondra struggled to rise.

Teresa grinned. "I'm spending the night. What would you like for supper?"

"Sleep," Dylan answered.

"With a side order of peace and quiet," Teresa tacked on.

Matthew started to whimper. Dylan chuckled ruefully. "Fat chance."

"Don't mention that awful word! I'm never going to fit in my jeans again!"

"Sondra, bitty as you started out, I'll bet PeeWee could wear them when he turns five. There's nothing wrong with a woman carrying soft curves. Gives a man something to hold onto."

"Oh, so now you're admitting that I've gotten fat and I was too scrawny at first. There's just no pleasing some people!"

He waited until she sat on her bed, then turned to his sister. "Teresa, talk some sense into her, will you? Oh, forget it!" Dylan stomped out of the house.

fifteen

Ranching—especially during the hot part of the year—demanded early morning work. Dylan had always been an early riser. The next day, he automatically woke up an hour earlier. He glanced over at the glowing numbers of his alarm clock and hopped out of bed. *If I hustle, I can have a bit of time with Sondra and PeeWee.*

He felt a bit self-conscious arriving at 5:00 a.m., but that initial wave of awkwardness disappeared when he heard the baby whimpering softly. A smile chased across his features. He wasn't going to be interrupting Sondra's precious sleep.

A blue diaper bag propped open her bedroom door. The white porcelain Guardian Angel nightlight glowed from the dresser, casting a soft light on the bed. Sondra lay curled on her side, snuggled under a pale yellow sheet. Oddly, Matt's soft whimpers didn't seem to be coming from Sondra's bedroom. Dylan frowned, moseyed over to the bassinet, and wondered where the baby was.

Teresa came in, Matt snuggled over her shoulder. Her oversized, OSU T-shirt made Dylan grin. "With pjs like that, no wonder Jeff let you spend the night over here."

His sister laughed.

Dylan pointed at Matt. "Hey, I'm hoping you and Jeff don't wait long before you have one of those."

"Hmm," a sleep husky voice whispered from the bed. "What's up?"

"Not what—who," Teresa said. "Your son started to wind up, so I changed him. Here you go."

Dylan nodded. "Breakfast of champions, huh?"

"Breakfast, lunch, dinner, midnight snack. . ." Sondra's voice sounded deep and slow. Waking up to that sultry purr would be the best alarm clock a man could ever have.

Teresa bumped him with her hip. "If you gather the eggs, I'll get breakfast going for us big people."

He wanted to protest that he'd come to see Sondra and the baby. . .but he stopped short. Even by the faint illumination of the nightlight, he could see the flush on Sondra's cheeks. *It's me*, he wanted to say. *Just me. Go on ahead.* . . But that wasn't right. He wasn't her husband. She had every reason and right to behave modestly. He spun around and headed for the coop.

❧

As he put a third egg in the basket, Dylan tried to decide how to proceed with Sondra. She was his—she simply didn't know it yet—and he wanted her to make that realization. If not now, *soon*.

How did a man let his woman ignore a love that was meant to be? How long was he supposed to let her live in solitude? He'd given her time to grieve. Now she needed time to recover physically and adjust to motherhood. *But when will it be my turn, Lord?*

He finished collecting the eggs and took them into the kitchen. Coffee trickled through the auto-drip. Diced ham, tomatoes, mushrooms, and grated cheese on the cutting board let him know Teresa planned to make her killer omelets.

"Stop looking like you lost the 4-H roping," she teased.

"Huh?"

"Oh, don't play stupid with me," she whispered. "I saw the look on your face when you brought Sondra home yesterday. You've got it bad, and I couldn't be happier."

"The lady's not exactly husband hunting."

"Mom said something when I was in high school that made me realize how I felt about Jeff. I'll pass her wisdom to Sondra some day in the future: 'No need to search the world over for a stallion when you already have one in the stable next door.'"

Dylan raised his brows a notch. "Run it by Sondra and let me know how she reacts."

"Time, Dyl. Give her time. By the way, know how a hen gets pecky when she's on the nest with her first brood and how protective she is with the chicks? Expect Sondra to do the same thing. She's going to be feisty and particular. Don't take it personally."

"How'd you ever get so smart?"

She cracked an egg into a blue earthenware bowl. "I was always the smarter one. Since I'm so brilliant, I'll toss one last jewel of wisdom at your big old boots. The one thing a woman can't resist is a man who's crazy about her kid."

Dylan smiled. Little Matthew was hot stuff. While the doctors stitched Sondra back up, the pediatrician had put PeeWee in his arms. He'd lost his heart in that instant. For a selfish moment, he'd cuddled Matt before scooting closer to Sondra so she could nuzzle his little face and croon to him.

Unaware of his thoughts, his sister continued, "I'm not going to think badly of you if you can't love Matt as your own, but if that would be the deep-down truth, don't mess with Sondra's heart."

"Soon as I admitted to myself that she's my One and Only, I knew Matt was part of the deal. I held him even before she did, and I swear on a stack of Bibles, in that instant, I claimed him as my own. He's a fine boy, and I'm gonna love being his daddy."

Teresa stood on tiptoe and kissed his cheek. "I was hoping you'd say that."

"So do me a favor. Don't offer to stick around after sunset. I'll take night shift."

"You got it."

Before Sondra had the baby, he couldn't possibly live here; but the situation had changed, and she needed help round the clock. It would be temporary, and folks could plainly see the necessity. No one in his right mind would question if any hanky-panky were going on.

Dylan widened his stance. "I'm going to work like crazy so this place turns even more of a profit than Miller required. I don't want Sondra thinking she had no choice but to marry a man who couldn't cut it, just so she could keep her home."

"Teresa?" Sondra's voice sounded from down the hall.

"Yeah?"

When Sondra didn't reply right away, Dylan went to see what she wanted. He got one look at her, clutching Matt and slumped against the wall over by the bedroom, and tamped down his alarm. He lengthened his stride. "Hey, there," he said softly, securely wrapping an arm around her waist and the other around the baby.

She sagged against him and confessed in a vague tone, "I'm a little dizzy."

Teresa slipped up behind him.

"Sondra, honey, give me the baby. I'll just ease him into Teresa's arms." To his relief, she cooperated. "Let's have you lie back down."

She didn't protest his plan. Her arm wound around his waist, and she shuffled a step. Her meek acquiescence bothered him. For her to yield without an argument went contrary to her nature. Dylan put her back to bed and quietly asked, "Are you having any other problems?"

"No." A hint of coloring started to suffuse her cheeks. Another few seconds passed, and though she didn't exactly look like her usual perky self, she revived a bit. "I just got up too quickly. I'm fine—I was worried that I might drop Matt."

Teresa laid the baby on the foot of the bed and sat next to him. "That could have been dangerous. I'll stay during the days for a week or two to help out."

Sondra took in a long, deep, choppy breath. Dylan watched as she blinked back tears. She nodded, though. "I'll keep Sondra company while you finish breakfast," he offered. "She needs some chow."

"I'm supposed to walk. I was going out to the kitchen."

Dylan scooted Matt across the bed and lifted him. Cradling him to his chest, he tried not to sound too bossy. If he started ordering Sondra from the get-go, she'd dig in her heels. "Walking's a good idea, but until you're not so shaky, Teresa or I will stay alongside you—like just now. Come Friday or so, you'll likely be able to tote PeeWee with you. Until then, what say you let us carry him, or you stick him in the bassinet and push it along like you did in the hospital? In a few weeks, you'll be a sassy ball of fire again."

"A few weeks!"

He toggled Matt back and forth a tiny bit. "Tell your mama to stop fussing."

For having ordered Sondra not to fuss about things, Dylan managed to do just that himself. He fretted all morning as he did his chores. There was a lot to occupy him, but he kept watch on the house. He normally wore a cell phone, and he'd checked the battery three times today, just to be sure it was fully charged. If Teresa needed help with Sondra or the baby, she could reach him in an instant.

He shook his head. Sondra likely felt hovered over. Still, the woman cherished the notion that she was capable enough to face everything on her own. Any reminders or hints to the contrary would get her back up.

Howie strode by and gave him a curt nod. Nickels leaned against a split rail fence, checking the frayed ends of a rope. He gave Dylan a cocky grin, then drawled, "Gonna get a terminal case of whiplash, looking back at the house."

Why deny it? I'm head over heels for Sondra, and little Matt's the cuddliest baby a man ever hitched over his shoulder. He let out a self-conscious chuckle. "Caught red-handed."

"Some things are worth catching and holding."

Dylan bent over and plucked a weed from the ground with studied nonchalance. "Teresa's spending days with Sondra to help with the baby. I'll be taking night duty."

"Boss, ain't a man on the spread who's gonna bat an eye over that. She needs lookin' after. Onliest one who's gonna kick up a fuss is her." He chortled softly. "When she's upset, she tosses pies. I reckon that ain't much of a deterrent to your plans."

By midday, Dylan couldn't take it anymore. He used the excuse of being nearby to invite himself in for lunch. "What are you doing?" He gawked at Sondra as she sat on the couch, fully dressed except for shoes.

She looked at him with slumberous eyes. "I had lunch."

"Dressed in your work clothes?" He scowled at Teresa. "What got into her?"

Teresa sighed. "She took a notion that she was going to go out to the coop and make sure the chickens got enough feed and water."

"You've got to be kidding me!"

Teresa shrugged. "I promised I'd see to it and convinced her to take a pain pill, so she'll nap for a while. Tuck her in bed, Dylan. She's too tired to pester. I'll get the baby."

"Sondra." He leaned down and burrowed his hands beneath her.

She tilted her head and rested it on his shoulder. "Hmm?"

"Settle down," he demanded as he lifted her. "No more cockeyed plans to traipse outside to do chores."

She wrapped her arms around his neck and actually snuggled closer.

Dylan already had a secure hold of her, but he curled her closer to his heart. His concern for her mingled with astonishment—not that he minded in the least, but she'd always been circumspect. His surprise must have shown, because Teresa gave him a nudge to set him into motion.

Dylan put Sondra to bed. Loath to break contact with her, he traced a rough fingertip down her nose. "Aren't you going to tell me what's going on?"

She blinked slowly and wet her lips. "There's so much to do."

"There's no denying that, sweetheart—but all you need to do is sleep and feed PeeWee. I'll handle the rest for a while."

He'd started to tuck a wild strand of her hair behind her ear, and she turned to his touch. He froze for a moment at the feel of her soft cheek against the backs of his fingers, then rubbed his knuckles back and forth in a tender caress. She'd needed him during her labor; now she turned to him. The woman had a knack for finding his empty spots and filling them, for making him feel essential—not just for the chores he could shoulder, but because something about him made her feel safe and cared for.

Dangerous ground. Setting yourself up for a big letdown, cowboy. If she doesn't cross the bridge from her past to your future, you're going to get burned.

sixteen

Late that evening, Sondra gingerly eased herself down into the rocking chair. Dylan scowled at her. "Don't take this the wrong way, but you don't look so red-hot."

She slowly wiggled from side to side to ease her weight deeper into the chair. "It's going to take time." Just when she'd gotten settled, the baby whimpered.

Dylan hopped up and got the boy. He made a comical face. "Caution! Toxic waste on board. Detour to the changing table."

Sondra manufactured a watery smile. It was downright funny seeing how Dylan handled the baby. "You're in Oklahoma, boy. You'll love the OSU Cowboys. Soon as you start talkin', I'll teach you to holler for the orange-and-white." The patter went on, regardless of Matthew's increasingly loud cry. It stopped as he presented a squalling, flannel-wrapped bundle to Sondra and announced, "He's on empty. Fill up his tank."

She accepted her son. "Thank you for everything, Dylan. As soon as things settle down, I'll make you a nice supper."

"Sounds to me like you need to be making *him* supper."

"Unh-huh. Good night, Dylan."

He sat down and gave her a mutinous look. "Good night? You think you're dismissing me?" When she nodded, he shook his head. "Not a chance. I'm not budging. Whether you like it or not, I promised to help you for a year. That promise extends on to the baby. Teresa is spending days with you until you heal. I'm spending the nights."

Sondra was sure she hadn't heard him correctly. "You're spending the night? You can't do that!"

"Just watch me."

She looked down at her crying son and then back at him, then blurted, "I don't want you to watch me!"

"Oh, stop fussing and feed the poor kid. You could've tossed a shawl or blanket over your shoulder and not shown a thing. It's not like I'm some kind of pervert or Peeping Tom." He heaved a longsuffering sigh and tromped out of the room.

Matthew snuggled close and nursed like a starving little piglet. He stopped crying, but Sondra started. She'd upset Dylan. She hurt. She was all alone, trying to rear a baby. Nothing was right. Tilting her head against the oak back of the rocker, she indulged in a fine fit of tears.

ð

A week later, Sondra walked across the living room and eased herself down onto a chair. "Dylan, I can't tell you how much I've appreciated all of the help—"

"If this is your 'I'm-fine-now' speech, forget it. You're nowhere near ready to handle things on your lonesome."

"You can't mean to stay here for another week!"

He plopped down on the sofa, put both stocking feet up on the coffee table, and gave her a mutinous look. "You still move like a rusty oil derrick and need the help. Now hush a minute. I want to hear the weather forecast."

Hush? He was telling her to hush in her own home and putting his big feet up on the coffee table as if he were king of the castle. Sondra did a slow burn. She was just about ready to give him a piece of her mind, but Matthew started to snuffle in the bassinet. Before she could even lean forward to get up, Dylan shot to his feet. He hurried to the baby and picked him up. For such a large man, he showed astonishing gentleness with Matt. Her gaze went from the man to the infant on his shoulder, then back again.

Dylan's eyes were shadowed with weariness, but he'd never once complained. He worked far too much, minding both ranches. On top of that he was babysitting the two of them and got up at least twice a night to help out.

At the moment, he wrinkled his nose and chortled softly. "You smell like a loaf of garlic bread. Your mama must have eaten the leftover lasagna for lunch!"

"I did," she confessed. "BobbyJo Lintz came over with her little boy. We shared it. Dylan, I can't believe it. Her baby is nearly five months old, and Matt is almost as big as he is!"

"Matt's gonna be a moose." Dylan laid the subject of their conversation on the couch and quickly changed his diaper.

The cable channel started showing grain, feed, and beef prices. Sondra had been absorbed with being overdue and with taking care of Matt. For the first time in two months, she stared at the figures on the television. "Dylan, look at those figures."

"I've been monitoring them."

She gave him a stricken look. "I'd better go review the books. Those are drastically different. If feed goes up higher and beef prices drop more, we won't turn enough of a profit!"

"Honey, the market fluctuates a lot. We'll ride it out."

"But this is Matt's home. We can't lose it."

"God and I'll get you through."

She gave him a pained look. "Dylan, I trust you to do your best. It's just that some things are beyond your control."

"That's why I gave God top billing. You're going to have to exercise your faith."

"Saying that is simple—doing it isn't!"

"Fretting won't change things." He yawned. "If all else fails, Miller gave us an escape hatch. We could always get married."

Sondra sucked in a sharp breath and stared down at Matt. By the time she gathered her scattered wits and found her voice, she rasped, "Dylan—"

She looked up and choked back a rueful laugh. Exhausted, Dylan had leaned back and fallen fast asleep.

❧

Over the next three months, the market bounced and

plummeted almost as often as Sondra's emotions. Dylan started spending the nights back at his own place, and she missed him terribly. Often, she invited him to stay for supper—he accepted, but almost as soon as he finished eating, he'd leave.

She longed for those quiet evenings they'd shared right after Matt was born and wondered if she'd done something to offend Dylan, but Teresa and Howie both commented on how Dylan was working hard to keep both spreads going. Sondra felt selfish for wanting more from him when he already gave so much.

Every Sunday, Dylan showed up in his truck, complimented her, and buckled the baby into the car seat. He drove them to church in her car—a committed act of a brother in Christ who wanted to help out. "Exercising faith," he called it.

What should have been her first anniversary arrived the week before Thanksgiving. She sat at the graveside and nestled Matt to her bosom. Confusion filled her. She still missed Kenny and ached for the loss she and her son had suffered.

Still, there was a niggling guilt, because she longed to have someone. Her brief time with Kenny had opened her eyes to the wonders of love—not just the physical fulfillment but the comfort of sharing the simple things of life.

Dylan's face flashed through her mind, but she shook her head. He'd already sacrificed too much for her. Oh, he did all of the ranch work, but even more—he'd eased her life and heart in countless ways. When their one-year partnership was over, she knew she was going to be bereft. *Lord, what am I to do? How will I survive that loss, too?*

⤞

The holidays arrived. Sondra went shopping and bought a calendar for the next year. She counted months since the beginning of May. *I've been here for seven months now, Jesus. There's so much I don't know still, and I don't think I can learn it all fast enough. Please give me a chance, though. Let us do well enough this year so I can keep the ranch.*

When she got to the gate of the Curly Q, Dylan met her. "Looks like you're dressed warm enough. How 'bout PeeWee?"

"He's all bundled up. Why?"

" 'Cuz we're going to go get his first tree."

She and Kenny had tried to get a tree, but the smell of fresh pine made her so sick, they'd gone back home. Kenny stopped along the way to buy a home pregnancy test. The next morning, they'd confirmed she was carrying a child.

Unaware of her memories, Dylan unlatched Matthew's car seat and transferred it to the jump seat of his pickup. "Do you have your heart set on anything particular?"

Sondra closed her eyes. "One that dusts the ceiling and is so wide, it fills the whole corner opposite the fireplace. No lights. Just ornaments."

A rough finger tickled her cheek. "Sounds like you've been dreamin' on this."

She blinked and bobbed her head. "Twenty-five years. I've never bought a tree."

He studied her for a moment and didn't ask questions. She appreciated that to no end. Sondra didn't want pity, and she'd blurted out her fantasy before realizing it would tattle about holidays best left forgotten.

"I know just the right place."

Fifteen minutes later, Sondra sat in his truck and frowned. "The hardware store?"

"Just you wait. In fact, stay put with PeeWee. I'll only be a second."

For all of the Christmases she'd spent as an unexpected and unwanted interloper in foster homes, Sondra determined to make Matt's holidays special. Having Dylan take them Christmas tree hunting meant the world to her. He insisted on carrying Matthew, brought along a camera, and snapped several photos. Instead of chopping down the tree, Dylan transplanted it into a huge pot he bought at the hardware store.

"Some things are meant to last," Dylan told her after finishing the task.

When they brought the tree back home, Dylan didn't leave. He stayed and helped her trim the tree with a box of beautiful, antique, hand-blown glass ornaments she'd unearthed in the attic. The newscaster started to discuss farm prices in the background, but Dylan switched off the TV and tuned the radio onto a station playing carols.

Everyone seemed to be in the Christmas spirit. A sprig of mistletoe was mysteriously tacked in the doorway to the barn. No one admitted to putting it there. Sondra glanced at it and forced a tight laugh. She hadn't been kissed in ages. As she walked under it, her heart did a wicked little skip. Dear mercy. . .she wanted to be kissed. Not just kissed, *kissed*. And at that moment, she knew exactly by whom: Dylan.

The realization floored her. A few months ago, he'd flippantly mentioned the marriage clause in the will. She'd been so scared about losing the home she needed so desperately for her son, she'd actually swallowed her pride enough to tell Dylan she'd be willing to get married—but he'd fallen asleep, and the words never came out. That would have been a friendship kind of marriage.

What she wanted now was entirely different. *I've fallen in love with him!* A kiss wouldn't be near enough. An amiable partnership wouldn't suffice. What she wanted was a happily-ever-after, madly-in-love marriage with Dylan. That realization stopped her cold. *Dylan's a good man. Honest, kind, generous. If he ever detects even a hint of my feelings, he'll ignore them—unless push comes to shove. If ownership of the ranch is at stake, he'll probably rescue Matt and me. . . .* But she didn't want that. She wanted him to love her back with all of the intensity she now discovered she held for him.

"Hey, now, what's that you got there?"

Howie's words jolted her. Sondra wheeled around. "Pecan snowballs and molasses pinwheels." She shoved the plate of cookies into Howie's hands.

Nickels swiped a pinwheel, wolfed it down, and reached for another. "I vow, this place don't much smell like a ranch; it smells like a bakery. Not that I'm complaining, mind you." He popped the next one into his mouth.

Dylan strode up. He helped himself to a snowball, but instead of eating it, he popped it into Sondra's mouth. "You're spoiling your men." The corners of his mouth crinkled. "I thought that was above and beyond the call of duty, and I just found out today that you've buried the men in the Laughing-stock bunkhouse under cinnamon rolls, strudels, cookies, and desserts, too."

She hastily swallowed the cookie. "We're—partners. Seemed fair to me. All of the men work hard. Matt and I want to show our appreciation."

Nickels pulled Howie back a few steps. Their boots crunched on the gritty soil. "Uhhh, boss?" They shot a meaningful look upward at the mistletoe. "Showing appreciation sounds like a mighty fine plan. Don't you think, Howie?"

"Sure enough. We elect you to be our um. . .whaddya call it?"

"Representative," Nickels filled in.

Sondra wished the ground would open up and swallow her. She felt a wave of heated embarrassment wash over her as Dylan studied the green sprigs dangling above them. He drew close, and she stopped breathing. He wrapped an arm around her. He smelled of soap and leather and man—a complex scent that enveloped her. Sondra's heart was about to pound out of her chest as his head dipped. . . . Then he ducked a bit more and pressed a kiss on Matt's downy head.

As he straightened, he stared into her wide eyes and ordered without looking behind him, "You men get back to work."

Sondra started to inch away, but his arm tightened. "I thought I was supposed to thank both of you."

If he kisses me, I'll never be able to face him again. He'll know. . . he'll know. Dylan kept an arm around her and used the other hand to tilt her face up to his. Every shred of her wanted to run; every bit of her wanted to raise up on tiptoe and. . . . She decided to play it safe. She popped up onto her tiptoes and gave him a hasty peck on the cheek.

His hold tightened, and his brows formed a stormy vee. "Just what was that?"

"A—a holiday kiss."

"Not on your life. That pathetic excuse for a kiss was something a maidenly great-aunt might concoct." His voice deepened to a husky, predatory purr. "This is a kiss."

Once again, his head dipped. His mouth slanted across hers. For all of the fire she'd seen in his eyes before she'd closed her own, he kept the contact tender. His lips brushed, teased, found a perfect fit. . .just as he shifted the baby between them slightly to the side, then cinched her so close, he left her breathless and dizzy.

Matt wiggled and cooed, jarring her from her abandoned reaction. She jerked away and couldn't bear to look Dylan in the eye. She'd just done what she most feared—lost control completely. A man didn't need any emotional attachment to enjoy a woman. What was an intense, emotional connection for her had been mere biology for him. *I've made a fool of myself in front of him. . . .* She craned her head to the side. *I hope the hands didn't witness that!*

"Sondra—"

"Matt just soaked me," she lied.

❧

Dylan watched her scurry back into the house. In all honesty, he felt like he had a whole boxful of crickets jumping in his belly. He'd nearly gotten lost in the moment. After waiting forever to kiss her, he'd wanted to cast aside all self-control.

Fighting that urge had to be the single hardest thing he'd ever done.

Good thing he did. For a glorious moment, she'd been with him. Then she jerked away like she couldn't stand his touch. Oh, yeah, she said Matt had wet her; but his own arm had been right beneath the little guy's bottom, and it was bone dry. Never before had Sondra lied to him. She made a very poor fibber, too. Her cheeks went fiery, and she avoided looking him in the face.

He hadn't taken any liberties. The woman had no call to be embarrassed because she'd responded so naturally to him. . . . *Unless she's not embarrassed, but ashamed because she still loves Kenny.*

Dylan grabbed a bale of hay and heaved it into a stall. Once, he'd resented Miller for saddling him with a city-girl and questioned God about why long-standing, charitable plans went awry. Now he understood Miller's matchmaking plans. . . . *But Almighty Father, why are You allowing me to be tempted with a woman who's so stuck on her lost love, she doesn't want me?*

seventeen

All her life, Sondra made it through by hiding her feelings. No one knew when things bothered her, and she didn't let them know when she was hurt. Now, it strained her to the limit to keep her emotions hidden—at least where Dylan was concerned. She left her heart unguarded, and it counted as the most foolhardy thing she'd ever done. It took all her courage to face him and feign nonchalance.

Dylan showed up every single day. His dedication and faithfulness were unquestionable. Sondra tried to find comfort in the fact that his work would help her keep the ranch. In truth, the intensity he now showed accomplishing the chores about the place troubled her greatly. She'd been painfully obvious in her attraction. Clearly, he was politely making it clear their partnership shouldn't have crossed the line. He was too much of a gentleman to say anything, but actions spoke louder than words. What good would it do if she kept the ranch but lost her friendship and partnership with her closest neighbor?

Another chilling thought occurred to her. Was she going to be able to keep the Curly Q? She pored over all of Miller's old books, and the facts shook her to the core. The price of beef was lower than it had been in the past four years, and due to meager rainfall, feed prices kept creeping higher. Were the dark shadows in Dylan's eyes strictly due to overwork, or was worry causing them?

As she walked to the henhouse, Dylan rode off. Nickels beat his gloves against his thigh, creating a small cloud of dust. He squinted at Dylan's back. "That man couldn't get more work done if he was twins!"

Sondra nodded somberly. "What can I do to help?"

Nicholson shrugged. "Dylan's got us all organized just fine. Seems to me you already have your hands full with a little one."

Her arms automatically curled around a little baby carrier she wore. She gave Nickels a wry smile. "Matt keeps me busy, but I'm getting pretty good at reaching around him. I'm tired of not pulling my weight around here."

"Ma'am, far as I can see you have no call to fret. Things go along at their own speed, and there's things on a ranch you can't change, hurry along, or make smell better."

After he strode off, Sondra shook her head. These men had seen the ups and downs of ranching. They were able to be more philosophical about the downturn in the market. Then again, even if the Curly Q didn't turn a profit, they could easily find a job elsewhere. She, on the other hand, stood to lose everything.

"I won't let that happen." She patted her baby on the back and vowed in an iron tone, "I'll do whatever it takes. We are not moving an inch."

❧

The kiss under the mistletoe had really done it. He knew they shared an explosive chemistry. Still, he didn't want Sondra thinking he chased after her for her land or livestock. If he got within three yards of her, he'd make a fool of himself because he'd likely grab her, kiss her silly, and confess his love.

Any fool could see she needed time yet. If he pressed her or started an obvious attempt at courtship, she'd bolt. One kiss, and she'd run away like a scalded cat. He ached for her, but for the sake of her peace of heart and his pride, he decided to back off. Day in, day out, he strove to keep some distance between them. He'd resolved to change that today. It seemed like a fair enough time to broach the topic of love and marriage, it being Valentine's Day and all.

Dylan planned each move. He'd pull out every stop, use

every trick in the book, and turn a stellar profit. That way, marriage wouldn't be an escape hatch she resorted to out of desperation. Once Sondra held the deed, he'd propose—with an offer up front of a prenuptial. That would prove he wanted her, not what she finally owned. Today, though, he'd start doing the little things that made a woman feel courted. . .like giving her a card. Flowers would be coming on too strong. Just one thing at a time.

He popped the card into his shirt pocket, rode over, and pulled to an abrupt halt in her barnyard. The place was quiet—eerily quiet. Pink-and-red iced doughnuts lay strewn and trampled on the ground.

❧

Sondra hit the automatic dial on the phone again. She twisted around and cranked the swing to keep Matt content, but with every ring and turn, her tension spiraled higher. "God, please help us."

"What's going on?"

She spun around. "Dylan! I've been trying to get you."

"What's going on?"

"Cows are down. Nickels said a dozen or more. South pasture."

He bolted out and vaulted onto Pretty Boy. Sondra ran to the door and called, "They already have the medical kit with them, and I called the vet."

After he'd gone, Sondra paced back and forth across the living room. Whatever it was, it was bad. She couldn't stay here when Matthew's future hung in the balance. She bundled Matthew up, strapped him into a car seat, and latched him into the jump seat of a pickup. They were halfway to the south pasture when her cell phone rang.

"Sondra, where are you?"

"By the old oak, turning toward the pasture. What do you need?"

"Rope and mineral oil."

"I have rope." In the distance, she saw him spin around and catch sight of her.

"You drove a trailer!" He hung up, and she wasn't sure whether he was glad or mad.

Dust swirled around the truck as she stopped. It didn't hide the appalling sight of cattle lying and staggering about. Sondra tore out of the cab. "What happened?"

"They ate mountain laurel." Dylan gestured toward clumps of shrubs and segments of branches along the fence and road. He didn't bother to hide the worry in his eyes or voice.

Not a day went by that Sondra didn't see Dylan and the men work hard. Never had she seen such grim determination or desperation. As they loaded several sick cows into the trailer, Dylan ordered, "Sondra, Milt came out in a jeep. Drive it to town and get as much mineral oil and lard as you can, then swing by the vet's. Once he's here, he'll call an order in to his assistant, and you can bring back everything."

After moving Matt to the jeep, Sondra called BobbyJo. "I need help. . . ."

By the time Sondra reached town, her new friend and Eva Nielson had two carts waiting outside the grocery store. "Here you go." BobbyJo tossed a box into the jeep. "I bought all their lard—seventeen buckets. Only nine bottles of mineral oil, though. Eva dashed to the drugstore and got two cases."

"Thank you both!"

"We're praying," Eva added.

"Please do. It looks bad." They loaded the jeep; then Sondra raced on to the vet's and back home.

⁂

Dylan paced the length of the barn and back again. Thirteen cows had died. He shook his head. *Lord, if I were a superstitious man, that would spook me. You're in control of this, but I don't understand why this happened or how we'll get through.*

The vet had just left after staying round the clock. His assistant would be here for the next shift. From the looks of it, one or two more cows wouldn't pull through. The other eighteen would. Between the ones they lost and the medical cost of saving the others, the ranch had just suffered a nasty blow.

Lord, I'm grasping at straws here. You know how hard I've been working. You know how important it is to me to reach that goal so Sondra won't just marry me out of pressure. With the feed prices high and beef prices low, it was already tight. This—well, this is a disaster. Four weeks. There are only four weeks until the lawyer figures out the profit margin. What am I to do?

"Dylan."

He wheeled around. Sondra walked toward him. Over the past thirty-six hours, she'd brought mountains of food and gallons of good, strong coffee to the barn. Instead of getting underfoot and pestering the vet with a bunch of questions, she'd seen to the matters that didn't disappear just because an emergency cropped up. Sweet little Sondra didn't even make a big deal of it, either. Pitching in came naturally to her—a trait Dylan admired to no end.

Others noticed, too. Edgar wasn't a man to do a lot of extra talking, but he'd come to the barn this morning. Sondra had gotten up early and already mucked the horses' stalls in order to free him up to do something else. He'd slapped Dylan on the shoulder and murmured, "You best better claim that gal soon, or I'm a-gonna."

Dylan folded his arms across his chest. "Over my dead body."

Edgar let out a rusty chuckle.

The moment of levity ended. More pressing issues were at hand. Dylan lowered his voice. "I want you to ride the fence. Keep close watch."

Solemnly nodding, Edgar rasped, "Gotcha."

Before Sondra arrived at the pasture yesterday, Dylan had ascertained the mountain laurel didn't end up in the pasture by accident. The sheer volume proved the wind couldn't have blown the heavy branches over the barbed wire fence. That's where it was, too—inside the pasture, not outside the wire, blown up by the fence. Someone intentionally set the poison in the pasture.

The hands knew it, too. Plenty of hot words and suspicions flew—until Sondra arrived. Dylan barely had a chance to order the men to keep their conjecture to themselves before she'd gotten out of the truck. Since then, they'd been circumspect. No use scaring the poor widow half out of her wits.

Sabotage. But who had a motive? More importantly, how could Dylan protect Sondra and the ranch from any further danger? Oblivious, she crossed the floor as if it were freshly swept linoleum instead of ankle-deep in cow patties. The tray she carried had several empty spots on it, telling him the men probably crowded around to grab sandwiches the minute she stepped foot out of the house. Even so, three big subs remained.

"I figured you must be starving."

As she drew closer, he squinted at the baby sling she used to carry PeeWee. It looked wrong.

"Chips and soda." She laughed weakly. "Teresa is at the house, watching Matt."

"Good." He took the tray from her and set it on a bale of hay.

"Middle one's roast beef and cheddar—your favorite."

Fishing into the roomy cloth sling, she pulled out a bag of barbecue chips and a soda.

"Mmm. Those are my favorites, too."

A smile sketched across her face. "I know."

She tilted her head toward the tray. "Roland, there's plenty more where this came from. Help yourself."

Nodding, the vet's assistant finished fiddling with an IV going to one of the cows. "Much obliged." He swiped a sandwich and soda, then cleared his throat. "They're doin' about the same. Mind if I go to the stables and look at the litter?"

"Go ahead." Sondra made a vague gesture. "The only one promised is the pup with white socks. You're welcome to any of the others."

"Thanks." He strode out.

Dylan took a bite. Her sandwiches always tasted great. This one might as well have been filled with sawdust. "Sondra, honey, I'm worried."

She motioned toward his sandwich. "Eat. Worrying won't change things."

He washed the bite down with soda.

She opened a soda and took a sip. "You're the one who's counseled me to exercise faith. I guess it's time for me to suggest it's your turn."

"Feeling sassy, are you?"

She lifted the can in a salute. "Probably. I'm a scrapper, you know."

"Yeah. It's an admirable quality. . .as long as you rein it in so you don't gallop straight into trouble."

"Trouble seems to find me often enough. I'm not about to issue any invitations!"

Studying her, he forced a smile. "Does it go with the hair?"

She smoothed back a few stray, twirly wisps. "Probably. Kenny's mom said God painted me with red neon to warn men off."

His last gulp of soda didn't stay down. Dylan choked and crushed the can in his fist. "What did she know, anyway?"

Sondra shrugged, but Dylan knew her too well to be fooled by the nonchalant action. The words stung. He refused to let them remain unchallenged. Sauntering over, he tossed aside the can and stared at Sondra's hair. Her eyes dilated with surprise.

"Neon red? The woman's color blind. It's mahogany. Rich, wonderful mahogany." He unfastened the barrette, threaded his hands through her hair, and growled, "Your hair doesn't warn a man off—it beckons him. Especially this man."

Her lips parted in surprise.

Dylan couldn't help himself. He'd longed to kiss her again, ever since that day under the mistletoe. Hands full of her hair, cradling her head, he lowered his head.

"Hey, boss!"

Sondra jerked away. His hands tangled in her hair, but she shook free, her cheeks scorched with color.

Nickels scuffled in. "Howie and me been think—oh." He halted, and his gaze shifted from Dylan to Sondra and back. "I'll get back to you later."

"Don't let me keep you." Sondra sidled away. "I was just bringing food. There's a sandwich. Help yourself."

Once she was gone, Nickels smirked. "She's cuter 'n a bug's ear when she's all embarrassed like that. Voice goes up a whole octave, too."

Dylan didn't say a thing.

Nickels grinned unrepentantly. "Only other time I've seen her do that was when she hit you with that pie. I suspect you got something even sweeter this time."

"You're wrong." Dylan glowered.

"Sorry, my timing stunk. So anyway, Howie and me were talking. We wondered who had it in for you or Sondra. We've gotta puzzle out who's got motive."

Dylan turned to the side and gulped soda. "If you have any ideas, let me know."

"Can't think of anyone who's got a bone to pick with you. As for Miz Thankful, well, it stretches my mind to imagine anyone bein' upset with her."

"She's a good woman." Dylan changed the subject. He didn't want to say anything more, but he'd already called the sheriff. Dylan could think of several people with a grudge— Miller's relatives.

The vet's assistant returned. Weary to the bone, Dylan grabbed a blanket and headed toward the ladder to the loft. He'd ascended three rungs when his sister's voice stopped him. "Dylan, the guest bedroom is ready for you. I stopped by your place and brought fresh clothes, too."

He looked down at her. "No thanks. I'll catch a few winks here."

His sister gave him a searching look. "Okay. Gotcha. Best for you to sleep here. Definitely best."

He didn't reply. Once he settled into a bed of hay and covered himself with the blanket, weariness washed over him in waves. *Sondra couldn't face me after that almost-kiss.*

eighteen

The printouts from the computer formed tidy stacks on the table. Dylan and Sondra sat side-by-side as she looked at the bottom line. It showed a deficit of five thousand dollars. Five stinking thousand dollars. If they couldn't account for those monies, the ranch would fall below the guidelines listed in Miller's will.

"So if we sell some steers right now, it still won't boost the profit?"

"No. They'll register at the same value as the price you'd get for them."

"If we sell off most of the hay we have on hand, that could raise some money."

Dylan grimaced. "Not enough. I've already cut it close on ordering. With feed prices at this level, I'd hoped to skim by."

She chewed on the end of a pencil. "I thought you did that to reduce the chances for any other fires."

He didn't answer.

Sondra's eyes narrowed. "That big roll of hay didn't have any reason to catch fire, did it? It wasn't green, so it shouldn't have gotten hot. And there wasn't a thunderstorm, either. You still don't say anything about the fire."

Dylan shoved the calculator across the table. The last figure on the sheet still told the same tale: They couldn't wrangle an honest way of reaching the goal.

"What do you want me to say? It's a bad situation."

"This may sound paranoid, but I wondered if someone set it on fire." She sucked in a quick breath and added, "And as long as I'm sounding like a nut case, I may as well confess that I suspect someone purposefully flung the branches into the pasture when the cattle got poisoned."

Dylan studied his knuckles. They'd gotten scraped yesterday. "What made you think that, and who'd do such a thing?"

"I don't know." She spread her hands wide. "You have to admit, it's pretty fishy that we've had two disasters in two weeks. There's not mountain laurel anywhere around that pasture, and that road's just a fire road that isn't on the map. It struck me odd at the time, but we were all so busy, I didn't say anything. Then the hay roll caught fire. I don't think it's a coincidence that it just happened to be the one next to the tractor barn."

"Good thing Luna spotted the smoke. Replacing machinery is costly."

"Exactly my point. This is the only ranch in the whole county that seems to be running into trouble." She shoved back an errant curl. "Well, that's not true. Compared to the Willards, I shouldn't complain at all. Those poor little kids lost their parents and home last week."

"That's not a good comparison. The tornado was a terrible tragedy, but at least we know what caused it. What's happened around here doesn't have an explanation. Who do you think would attempt to sabotage the Curly Q?"

She shrugged. "I don't have any enemies. And everyone in the community goes out of their way to sing your praises. The thing I keep coming back to is, if we don't turn enough of a profit, the ranch gets sold."

"But who benefits from that? None of Miller's relatives gets a cent if we fail. A developer does."

"I told you you'd probably think I'm acting paranoid. I can't help it." She blinked madly. "My son's future is at risk."

He cupped her face and rubbed away the tears that began streaking down her cheeks. "It doesn't have to be, Sondra. Miller provided another way."

She smiled bravely. "You're right. Miller provided fifteen thousand in this eventuality. That'll help Matt and me get started."

"Don't be ridiculous. Fifteen won't cover rent and child care for the first year." His steady gaze held hers. "We'll get married."

"From the very start," she said unsteadily, "we agreed that wasn't an option."

"We were total strangers back then. We've had almost a year to get to know each other. We're far more compatible than either of us suspected."

She stayed silent.

"We just finished tallying it up again. I'm sorry I didn't pull you through."

"Dylan, I've never once doubted your commitment or generosity. No one else would have worked as tirelessly or diligently. It's not your fault."

"But I can make it right. Marry me, Sondra."

❧

Matthew started crying. Sondra wanted to wail right along with him. She pushed away from the table. "We have one more week."

"Things won't be any different next Friday."

"Please excuse me." She hastened out of the room and headed for the nursery. Sondra stood in the shaft of moonlight flooding the nursery and swallowed back her tears as she changed Matt's diaper. A year and a half ago, she'd been planning her dreams-come-true wedding to Kenny. Now, she was seriously contemplating pledging her hand to a man who never once mentioned love in his proposal. Her heart ached.

Was it grief for having lost Kenny? Was it sadness that Dylan didn't truly love her? She couldn't untangle the knotted threads of emotions. Having someone to help her rear Matt would be an answer to prayer. She was so afraid of being a single parent.

That's not a good enough reason to get married.

If she didn't marry him, she and Matt would lose their home and precious time together. She'd need to go back to work as a teacher and leave him with a babysitter each day. *That's a good enough reason for me to marry—but I'm just using Dylan. . .and that's wrong.*

She did care for him—deeply. She'd called it love, but that seemed impossible to believe. How could she have already opened her heart and soul to another man? *But I have.*

Matthew snuffled, then let out a little squeak that quickly increased in pitch. A floorboard creaked as Dylan came in. "He thinks it's time for a snack, huh?"

"Actually, he's been sleeping through the night." She fastened up the snaps on the pale green sleeper and lifted Matt.

Dylan took the baby and surprised her by sitting on the ottoman in the moonlight. He patted the rocking chair in a silent invitation for her to join him. The soft, almost bluish light illuminated the patience on his weary face.

I want my son to have this man for his daddy. . .and I want him for myself, too. Sondra sat and rocked in pensive silence.

Matt snuggled into Dylan's arms, gave him a sleepy smile, and yawned. Dylan's callused hand smoothed errant baby curls. "Sondra, I'll be steady and true. We can build something good out of this. I don't want you thinking I'm doing this for the land or livestock, so I'll sign a prenuptial."

"No." She shook her head adamantly. "If we do this, it's because we plan to really make a go of it—not just to weather a bad turn in the market and a pair of ill-timed mishaps. Stability and commitment are too important. Signing papers like that presume the marriage will fail. If you have any notion that you'll want to divorce in the future, then I'm not going to even consider this far-fetched plan."

"It's not far-fetched, honey pie. It's real as real can be. A forever kind of deal."

"We still have a week, Dylan. You need to use the time to consider what you're proposing."

"I know exactly what I'm doing. It's the right thing, Sondra. Trust me."

The right thing. Why did something so right for her seem so wrong? *Because he's being gallant. He's offering me his hand, but his heart's not involved.* His scuffed work boots grew blurry. Sondra looked up and fought to paste on a smile as she blinked away the tears. He looked so earnest. *Lord, is this Your will? You've put the desire in my heart. With time, will You teach Dylan to love me?* They sat only two feet apart, but it felt like an unbridgeable gulf.

"Exercise faith." His words whispered across the distance.

Nothing he could ever say or do would have answered her troubled heart and mind better. Silence stretched as they studied each other in the muted light. "Do you mind if we get married in the pastor's study instead of city hall?"

"There's a pretty little prayer chapel tucked away behind the main sanctuary. If it's all the same to you, I'd like to say our vows there."

A church wedding. Sort of. Well, it was fitting. God brought them together, and Sondra was taking a huge leap of faith in marrying Dylan. She desperately wanted the Lord's blessing on their union. "I'd like that."

"Do you want me to surprise you with a ring, or would you rather go shopping with me and chose something?"

"Dylan, we don't need to spend a lot of money on a ring. I—"

"Whoa." He held up a hand. "Hold it right there. This might not be one of those Valentine's-y kind of high school romances, but some things aren't negotiable. This is one of them. You'll have a nice ring. Pretty, like you." He winked. "That's something I'll teach little Matt. Anything worth doin' is worth doin' right. No sliding by."

Not a romance. Her nails dug into the wooden arms of the chair as she leaned away from him. The rocking chair tilted back, then arced forward again—toward Dylan, then went back again. *Together, apart. Together, apart. Just like us.*

Dylan rose and tucked Matt into his crib with ease, then turned to her. He took her hand and helped her from the rocking chair.

She fought the urge to lean into his strength. She'd done almost no dating at all until she met Kenny, and he'd been at an easy-to-reach level. Dylan was huge with brawny shoulders and arms from his heavy work. Long, toned legs gave him towering height, too. Dylan had a way of engulfing her with his presence and making her feel secure. Too secure.

His callused hand enveloped hers, wouldn't let go. His other hand slowly tilted her face to his, and his voice went as rough as his hand. "Let's seal it with a kiss."

❧

Dylan strode up to the two-story clinic and would have taken the stairs, but a cordon across it warned, "Wet Varnish." The pungent smell of fresh varnish permeated the lobby as he wrinkled his nose and jammed the UP button on the elevator. He was alone in the stainless-steel-lined car and did a quick check to make sure he didn't look too shabby. One glance at his reflection told him his hair needed taming in the worst way.

He got out of the elevator car, glanced about Doc's waiting room, and spotted Sondra in a mustard-colored plastic chair. She held the baby to her shoulder, and her head rested back against the wall. Her eyes were closed; her lips thinned.

"Here, Sondra, I'll take the little guy."

Her eyes flew open. "Dylan!"

He leaned forward and brushed a kiss on her cheek, then swiped Matthew from her. "Figured we'd make this a family trip."

"You're sick?"

Her concern warmed his heart. "No, honey. We need to have Doc do blood tests for the marriage license. I told Nickels to go on ahead. After we pick up the marriage license, I'll drive you home."

"Okay. Thanks."

Her face still looked strained. *She really doesn't want to marry me.*

The corner of her mouth twitched. "I hate this. Matt's going to get more shots today."

Relief flooded Dylan. *So at least it's not just the wedding; it's not just me.* He tickled her cheek. "You gonna cry more than he does?"

"Can't say I'm not tempted."

"Can't say I'll cope any better." Dylan winced theatrically and cuddled Matt closer. "Nothing worse than someone pickin' on a kid. You might have to hold me back so I don't grab the syringe and toss it out the window."

Sondra let out a small laugh. Her features finally eased, making the nonsensical conversation worthwhile. Dylan grinned. He knew he'd turned into a fool for love, and he didn't mind in the least.

A short while later, Dylan kept his left hand on the steering wheel and stuck out his right forearm. "You've kissed little PeeWee's boo-boo a hundred times or so. Don't I get a kiss for my boo-boo?"

"Boo-boo?"

The corner of his mouth kicked up. "What else do you call 'em?"

"Ouchies!"

Dylan chuckled. "I see. After you kiss my ouchie, it's plain we're going to have to have a serious talk."

"Dylan—"

"Kiss first," he ordered.

Her lips glanced off his arm—like a butterfly barely lighting before flitting away. A second later, she ripped off the tape and cotton ball.

"OUCH!"

"Told you it was an ouchie!"

He cocked a brow and muttered, "I'll give you that one."

Sondra took a deep breath and let it out. "Dylan, we do need to talk seriously."

"Unh-huh." He agreed gravely. "I wouldn't have it any other way, because I'm not about to have you teaching our boy sissy terms for things. As far as I'm concerned, it's nonnegotiable. He's going to learn the manly way of sayin' what needs to be said. . . . Take, well, say for instance, him needin' to go see a man about a horse. . . ."

Giggles spilled out of Sondra. "See a man about a horse?!"

"No better way to say it." He punctuated his pronouncement with a definitive nod. "You get ouchie. I get that." His heart started to beat a million times a minute as he added, "There's something else I get. Kenny will always be his pa, and I won't challenge that one bit; but I'm the man who'll teach him to walk and ride, and I'm to be called his daddy."

He'd never risked so much, put his heart on the line like that. In one fell swoop, he'd managed to demand a place in Sondra's life—an official place as her husband and the daddy to her precious son. Never once had he dared to think of himself as lucky enough to find a woman to love with all his heart and soul. Now, with Sondra and little Matthew, he hungered so badly to have them be his very own, he risked grabbing for the future. She might think it was a business arrangement, but Sondra was a woman with a big heart. Given enough time, she'd come around. *Please, God, let it be true.*

His voice went rough as he pledged, "I'll be a good daddy to him. You have my word on it. I'll be firm, but fair. I'll protect him and teach him."

Say something, Sondra. . . .

"If we ever have other children, little Matt will still be our firstborn and every bit as much mine—I wouldn't be the kind to shove him off to the side in favor of them."

Her hand squeezed his elbow. "You'd never show favorites, Dylan. I know that."

He shot her a quick look.

"I suffered that fate, and if I thought for one second you'd shortchange Matt, I'd walk away."

"Then take off your boots, honey, because you aren't going anyplace but home."

nineteen

"Come on over here and sit down for a minute."

Dylan's invitation surprised her. Sondra figured the minute they got home, he'd rush off. Instead, he'd popped Matthew into the baby swing and taken a seat on the couch. She took a few steps closer. "What is it?"

He grinned. "Well, at least you followed half of my directions." He tugged her down beside him, reached over, and took her left hand in his. Slick as could be, he took a ring and slipped it onto her fourth finger. She hadn't gotten her wedding ring repaired yet, so the finger was bare. He adjusted it so the solitaire glittered.

"Dylan—"

His hand came up, lifted her chin, and his lips met hers in a soft, warm kiss. For this being a business agreement, it felt so good, so real. He cupped her cheek and wound his other arm around her shoulders so she was entirely in his keeping—and she could do nothing other than melt as Dylan continued to brush his lips gently across hers. He murmured something against her cheek, but her pulse thundered too much for her to distinguish the words.

Dylan whispered against her temple, "I'm ready for the two of you. You're a special woman, and I'm praying for God to bless us."

Click, clack, click, clack. . . . Matthew's baby swing beat out a rhythm.

"I'm praying, too." What more could she say? *I'm asking the Lord for you to fall in love with me? I'm begging God that you won't feel this is a big mistake someday?*

"Do you want us to live here or over at the Laughingstock?"

Looking around, she fought a sense of dread. The last thing Sondra wanted to do was pack up and move again. But that was his home. He'd grown up there, and she'd been here just shy of a year. He was already making all of the sacrifices. "Don't you want to live there?"

His arm tightened about her, and she rested her head on his shoulder. "If it's all the same to you, this place is bigger and you have it all fixed up the way you like. Teresa and Jeff are renting a dinky apartment. They'd probably jump at the chance to live over at the Laughingstock."

"I'm eavesdropping," Teresa sang from the other side of the screen door. "If you're really making the offer, we accept."

"Come on in." Sondra eased free from Dylan's hold.

"Dylan called from town and asked me what size ring you wore," Teresa bubbled. "I'm so excited for the two of you! I came by to help you plan everything."

Dylan stood. "I need to get back to work." Instead of just leaving, he tilted Sondra's face to his. One hard, quick kiss, and he was gone.

"Wow." Teresa laughed. "Let me see your ring."

After Teresa admired the engagement ring, she asked, "What are you wearing for the wedding?"

Sondra let out a yelp. "I don't have anything!"

Teresa laughed. "Of course not. You had a baby. Things change after that. Besides, you need a new dress for your wedding. I know just the thing, too." Teresa led her into the office and seated her at the computer. "Watch." Seconds later, she entered a Web site address.

"This is for bridal gowns!"

"That's exactly what you are." Teresa gave her a stern look. "You've done this before, but Dylan hasn't. He even took his suit to the dry cleaners."

"He hates wearing suits!"

"He did it so he'd look handsome for you. You need to look pretty for him." Teresa's fingers flitted over the keyboard.

"You don't have to wear yards of white satin and lace, but look here."

"Those are too fancy."

"Wait a minute." Teresa continued to scroll down the page. She glanced up for a second. "It'll just be his hands and yours there. Probably thirty guests in all—not a huge gathering, but they're the men who owe their livelihoods to the both of you."

"I just thought it was going to be us and a couple of witnesses."

"Nonsense. Forget that old saw about the wedding being for the bride. It's for everybody, because they all want a chance to celebrate. You belong together—I've seen it from the day I walked into your bedroom and saw him cradlin' you on his lap like you were manna from heaven."

Had Dylan been attracted to her all of this time? *No. Impossible. I was pregnant!*

Teresa squinted at the monitor. "What about maybe wearing something with a hint of apricot? With priority delivery, your wedding dress will be here tomorrow."

Sondra bumped her out of the way and found the perfect dress. *Maybe, if we really do this up right, Dylan will—*

"Here. Order by phone." Teresa nudged the phone closer. "See if they have it in a petite, or we'll need to order super-high heels so the hem doesn't drag."

Placing the order, Sondra tried to tamp down the spurt of hope she felt. The years of shuffling from one home to the next taught her love didn't blossom just because people lived under the same roof. *But God can work miracles. . . .* She called a caterer and ordered a wedding supper, then called the florist.

Lord, I'm doing my part. I'll trust You to work on him.

⊷

Dylan's breath hitched. The last rays of sunlight spilled through the stained glass and gave a jubilant look to the church. Candles glowed. Two discreet flower arrangements dressed up the altar. Good thing the pastor's wife had insisted on them using the church instead of the little chapel. Folks sat squished together in the pews because word got around. Every last hand from both ranches, neighbors, the friends Sondra had made, and their church family all showed up.

Strains of the traditional Wedding March started, and the guests stood. For a moment, Dylan couldn't see Sondra at all. Nickels walked her down the center aisle, looking proud as could be. Dylan subtly rocked forward onto his toes to see his bride.

She looked beautiful. For a moment, he thought she'd come to him wearing white lace. As she drew closer, he realized the antique-looking dress was creamy, but she wore a peachy-colored slip underneath. It looked soft and feminine—not fussy and overblown—but just right. Bridal enough to let her look like she wanted to get married—not so fancy that he felt uncomfortable. She had a knack for doing things perfectly.

She'd woven a few sprigs of baby's breath into her fire-bright tresses. Teresa had clued him in about buying a bridal bouquet. The roses shook a bit as Nickels placed Sondra's hand in his.

Don't be scared, honey. I'll be a good husband to you.

At their request, the pastor kept things simple. Dylan warmed her cool hands in his as he said his vows. Her voice faltered slightly, but she kept her big, green eyes on his face the whole time. Once the words were said, she smiled. Dylan's tension drained away. *You're mine now.*

"You may kiss your bride."

He kissed her with a joy he'd never felt before. The scent of her roses and the glow of the candles faded away until Matthew cried.

"I'd like to present Mr. and Mrs. Dylan Ward."

Dylan motioned to Teresa. She came to the altar and gave him Matt. He kept one arm around Sondra and cradled Matt in his left arm as he tacked on, "And their son."

Everyone clapped. Music played, and he led her back down

the aisle. As they stepped out of the door, into a small grass courtyard, he saw Miller's brother.

Edwin. He'd been skulking around. The sheriff suspected he'd been behind the sabotage. In fact, they'd discovered Edwin had invested his money in the Tuttlesworth developing company that stood to buy the land. Still, they couldn't find any concrete proof against him.

Dylan quickly turned so Sondra wouldn't catch sight of him. Anger surged. She and Matthew were his family, and he'd protect them and their land with everything he had in him. Nothing was going to ruin their wedding day. *What God hath joined together, let no man put asunder. . . .*

❧

Finally, they were alone. Well, not exactly alone. Matt let out a happy squeal. Grateful for his interruption, Sondra let out a nervous laugh. "I hope you're used to his noise already. If anything, he's starting to make a lot more of it as the days pass."

Dylan chuckled as he pulled off his tie. "I'll get him. You probably want to change into something more comfortable."

She froze at that phrase. Did he mean. . . ?

"Um, scratch that. I mean, well, how about if we opt for jeans? I hate wearing a suit. Your dress is beautiful, but it can't be your first choice of something to lounge around in."

Her shoulders slid back down with the silent sigh of relief. Sondra sidled out of the room, into the master bedroom. She shut the door very quietly and pressed her back to it. *This is so awkward.*

Matthew cooed loudly from his room next door. Dylan's deep chortle followed. "Hey, PeeWee, where are your jeans?" Drawers slid open and banged shut.

Sondra thought about calling out to tell him they were in the second dresser drawer. Instead, she headed toward her closet and grabbed a pair for herself. Baggy ones. Not that any of her jeans were tight, but she didn't want anything even vaguely form-fitting. Unzipping her dress required gymnastic stretching and wiggling. Once it fell into a pool around her ankles, Sondra looked down at the frothy lace and peach satin. Dylan liked her wedding gown. She'd get it dry-cleaned and keep it special—maybe wear it on their first anniversary.

Ha. First anniversary. I'm thinking of twelve months from now, and I can't even imagine how I'm going to make it through the next twelve hours!

A daisy-printed tee shirt and jeans. Her hair clipped back into a bouncy ponytail. Sondra studied herself critically in the mirror. She looked. . .casual. Comfortable. At ease. Appearances certainly were deceiving. She felt all knotted up inside. The man she'd fallen in love with and married didn't love her. Without a heartfelt commitment, how could they share a wedding bed?

We should have discussed it before now. A three-day engagement definitely qualified as whirlwind, but they should have covered that important topic before now.

Only they hadn't.

Sondra whispered a prayer for help, then went in search of her husband.

"We're ready for you." Dylan plunked a bowl of ice cream on the table. Matt and I decided the dinky slices of cake weren't enough to fill even a little cowhand like him."

"That bowl is big enough for Matt to swim in!"

"Yeah." Dylan pouted. "I looked for a bigger bowl, but I couldn't find one."

"It's the biggest I have!"

"You'd better buy a decent-sized one with one of the gift certificates we got."

"The only thing bigger would be a hot tub!"

"Good thinking." He pulled an aerosol can from the refrigerator, shook it, and squirted whipped cream atop what looked like an entire half-gallon of fudge brownie ice cream.

Matt banged his palms on the plastic tray of his high chair

and let out a stream of gibberish.

"Gotcha, PeeWee." Dylan pivoted and squirted a frothy pile of whipped cream onto the tray. "Snack time."

"Snack?" Sondra gasped. "That's the size of the iceberg that sank the Titanic!"

He added more. "Never let it be said that I skimp."

Sondra laughed in disbelief. Getting into the spirit of things, she sat down, swiped the big bowl, and gave Dylan a wink. "So where's *your* ice cream?"

He leaned against the counter and smirked. "Where's *your* spoon?"

"Oops." He blocked the silverware drawer.

"I think we have a stand off."

Easing back, Sondra gave him a "wanna-bet?" smile. Swift as could be, she opened the dishwasher and pulled out a spoon. When she turned back around, the playful victory she felt turned into disbelief.

Dylan took advantage of the brief second while her back was turned to grab a big serving spoon from the ceramic jar by the stove. He'd scooped a big chunk from the bowl.

"Community property." He looked downright smug as he took a lick.

"Uh, Dylan?" She stared at the front of his shirt. "I don't want to rain on your parade, but you got the slotted spoon."

"Yah, yah, yah, yah!"

Dylan swiped a finger of ice cream and dabbed it on Matt's cream-covered chin. "You have no room to talk. Besides, we men have to stick together."

"With that mess, you're guaranteed to stick!"

The kitchen rang with his booming laughter. Sondra leaned back in her chair and let out a sigh of relief. At least for now, they'd gotten past the awkwardness. *Lord, please let everything else work out this easily!*

twenty

Dylan stood by her side as she tucked the baby into his crib for the night. She covered Matthew with one of the blankets made from Kenny's shirts. *Well, that really puts me in my place. As if I needed any reminder that she still loves her late husband.*

He took a chance and slipped his arm around her waist. "What about bedtime prayers?"

She blinked up at him in surprise. "Really? This early? I mean, I pray for him, but well. . ." The corner of her mouth twitched nervously. "When I was a kid, no one ever said bedtime prayers. I sort of thought maybe you were supposed to start that when they could listen to a Bible story or something."

"One of my earliest memories is of my dad kneeling by my bed." Dylan kept his arm about her and reached over the rail to finger Matthew's soft baby curls. "As the years passed, I always loved having the security of him or mom praying with me. Anything—big or small—got mentioned in those prayers. I have a distinct memory of Dad checking under the bed and Mom looking in the closet because I was so sure there were monsters. Even when they didn't find one, Dad prayed for God to set angels about me so I'd be safe. It's how I learned God cared and listened to all of my concerns."

"Oh, Dylan. I'd love to have Matt grow up with that assurance."

"Then let's start having bedtime prayers with him."

For all the times he'd heard Sondra say grace at a meal, Dylan was unprepared for her prayer over her son. Those brief, sweet moments gave him a glimpse of her heart. After she finished, he prayed, too.

Sondra left on the nightlight. Dylan filed that detail away for future reference. Little things like that made a big difference to a kid. And to his mom. Especially to a mom like Sondra. She tried so hard to make everything perfect for her son—as if she had to make up for Kenny not being there and for her own poor childhood.

Well, he won't have Kenny, but he has me.

"That was so sweet, Dylan. Matthew's first bedtime prayer. I'll have to record it in the baby book."

"That baby book must weight a ton by now."

"Haven't you seen it?"

"Nope."

Sondra scurried over to the cabinet. "You've got to see it. Really."

Dylan sat on the couch, figuring a groom ought to get to cuddle a bit with his bride on their wedding night. She carried a big, baby blue album over and sat close enough to have their elbows brush.

Dylan wrapped his arm around her and dragged her tight against his side. "There. Much better. Now we can lay it across our laps. That thing is huge. Lookie there." Dylan chuckled as he ran his fingertip around the border of baby animal stickers she'd used to embellish the first page that held Matthew's birth certificate. "You got downright fancy on this page." The only thing that would have improved that page would be if his own name were listed as "father."

"Oh, you just wait." Sondra turned the page.

Pictures from the hospital filled the pair of pages. He'd taken those pictures himself, since she'd been so tired and weak. She'd filled in a little square with Matt's vital statistics. Dylan tapped it. "You thought he was so big, and he was just a tidbit."

"I know." She turned the next page. Dylan stared.

She'd blown up one photo to the full size of the page—it was nothing but Matt's bitty little hand resting in Dylan's.

That photo now took on special significance.

Sondra shifted, and the caption she'd penned came into view. It was a line from a song they sometimes sang in church. *I am weak, but he is strong.* Below that, she'd written more. *God provides, Matt. He brought a kind, capable man into our lives who helped us through and cared.*

"It's true," she said in a shaky voice. "You've been wonderful, Dylan. I can't ever thank you enough or repay—"

He didn't want her gratitude; he wanted her love. Dylan shut the book and turned to her. She'd stopped speaking at his abrupt action, and her eyes widened in surprise. "Let's get something straight. Being married to you suits me just fine. I don't want to hear how thankful you are."

"Because I'm not Thankful anymore—I'm Ward, right?"

He nodded emphatically. "You got it." *Lord, I prayed that tonight would go well. You're coming through like gangbusters. Please give me the strength and ease us through this next topic.* Jutting his chin toward the suitcase by the door, he said, "I already carried my other suitcase into the spare bedroom. I know we touched on having kids some day, but well—" He paused, hoping she'd want him, want a real marriage, but she tensed and didn't say a word. Her eyes darkened and filled with tears. No way was he going to take her to bed unless she loved him.

"I—" He cleared his throat. "I—reckon the first one we have won't be another honeymoon baby."

Silently, she nodded.

They gave each other a chaste hug in the hallway, then went to separate rooms. Dylan stared at the dinky twin bed as he unsnapped his shirt. He'd pledged himself to Christ and had waited all these years for his wedding night. So here it was. But he was alone, and the woman he loved couldn't bear the thought of sharing a bed with him.

❧

They sat across the breakfast table in aching silence. The empty inches between them at the table might have just as well been miles. Sondra poked at the runny yolk of her egg, and Dylan gulped down scorching hot coffee. The idea of starting each day of the rest of her life awkwardly searching for something to say made her shudder.

"You okay?"

She forced a smile. "I, um. . .usually don't eat my eggs over easy. I wasn't paying attention."

"Listen, you don't need to get up this early to make breakfast."

Squaring her shoulders, Sondra said, "Hold it right there. As I recall, you're the one who recently said anything worth doin' is worth doin' right. No sliding by."

"Oh, ho. So you're tossin' my words back at me, are you?"

Her fork skidded through the egg and scraped on the plate. She couldn't bear to look at him as she mumbled, "This might not be one of those Valentine's-y kind of marriages, but some things aren't negotiable. This is one of them."

"Fine." He rose from the table, stuck his plate in the sink, and popped a Cheerio into Matthew's mouth. Without another word, he left.

Sondra dumped her eggs down the sink and let out a shaky breath. *Lord, I don't know what to do. Give me strength and help me to become the wife Dylan needs.*

The next day, they barely spoke. Everything was ultrapolite. Only the most essential things were said, and the most necessary ones went left unsaid. They tucked Matt into his crib and prayed over him, then sat in the living room where the only sounds were the rustling of the newspaper and the tick of the clock. At bedtime, Dylan slept in the guest room again.

Over the following week, he was his usual, helpful self. Sondra pasted on a smile and tried to do as much as she could around the house. She paid bills, sewed buttons on Dylan's shirts, made nice meals, and set about trying to blend in some of the things from Dylan's house so this place would feel more like home.

More like home? This wouldn't ever be his home. He already regretted marrying her. She sat down to rock Matt and blinked back tears. Again.

The porch screen banged. "I brought over another box of Dylan's stuff," Teresa said. "I'll stick this on your bed."

"Just leave it there." Desperate to keep Teresa from knowing Dylan wasn't sharing her room, Sondra blurted out, "Dylan will carry it back later."

"Okay." *Thud.* The box landed on the floor. "I'm moving our stuff into the Laughingstock. If you need something, call, and I'll see if I can find it. I'm telling you, Dylan was alone in that house for six months, and everything's in the wrong place."

"New isn't wrong; it's just different."

"You tell her, honey," Dylan said from the doorway.

"Oh, boy. You're just like Mom and Dad were—the united front, absolutely indivisible."

"Yup." Dylan jerked his thumb toward the box. "What's in that?"

"Stuff from the closet shelf. Jeff just dumped it all in there for me."

Sondra gave her a mock look of outrage. "You have no room to talk about our teamwork. You and Jeff are quite a pair yourselves."

"I seem to remember you having a hand truck. Mind if I borrow it?"

"Help yourself. It's out in the barn." Sondra stood and slipped Matt into his playpen. "I've used it to move bales of hay, so you might want to hose it off."

"Okay. Why don't you come over tomorrow and take whatever you want? There's some stuff in the kitchen you might like that belonged to Mom or Grandma."

"Don't you want it?" Sondra couldn't hide the surprise in her voice.

"I took a few things that had sentimental value to me, but you're family, and the two of you ought to have some of it, too."

Dylan slid his arm around Sondra's waist. "Sure. You took Mom's china. Maybe we'll take Grandma's. There's this huge old turkey platter. . . ."

"Oh, boy. He's going to start drooling any minute." Laughing, Teresa gave them a quick hug. "I'm getting out of here. See you tomorrow!"

Dylan hefted the box and carried it off to the guest room. When he sauntered back in, he took one look at Sondra and silently grabbed the tissue box. Setting it closer to the rocking chair, he somberly looked into her brimming eyes. He sat down heavily on the coffee table, leaned forward so his forearms rested on his thighs, and let his hand dangle. "Guess we'd better talk."

Sondra slipped into the rocking chair. *If only he'd wrapped his arms around me or wanted to sit beside me on the couch.*

He waited a long second, then said very quietly, "I can't live like this."

twenty-one

Sondra looked at him and tried to choke back a sob.

"I'm not good at this stuff," he rasped.

Before he could say more or she could respond, the phone rang. And rang. And rang. Neither of them moved. The answering machine clicked.

"Dylan? Sondra? This is Troy Upton. I need you to come down to the sheriff's office."

Dylan heaved a sigh and headed for the phone. Sondra listened as he spoke. The conversation was short and cryptic. When he hung up, he came back to her and rubbed his forehead. "Something's up, but I'm not sure what. We need to go there now."

Sondra threw a few essentials into a diaper bag while Dylan washed up. They didn't do much talking on the road. Sondra kept hearing his words echo in her mind. *I can't live like this. . . .* She glanced at his profile, then stared out the window. *God, what should I do? Love isn't supposed to hurt like this.*

As he pulled into a parking place, Dylan murmured, "I'll grab PeeWee."

Diaper bag slung over her shoulder, Sondra walked alongside Dylan down the sidewalk to the sheriff's office. Dylan held the heavy door, and Sondra slipped inside. He always minded those simple courtesies, and it made her feel like a queen. "Thank—" Her voice died out, and she froze in place.

Dylan slid his warm palm to the small of her back and stood beside her.

"What's he doing here?" Sondra inched closer to Dylan as

162

she tried to focus anywhere other than on Miller's brother, who sat in a room off to the side.

"I have a feeling we're about to find out."

"Hi, Dylan," the receptionist said. "Y'all go on back to Troy's office."

Sondra looked around, and Dylan slipped his arm around her waist. "This way." He led her down a short hall and into an office. "What's up, Troy?"

"I need to ask you folks a few questions." As soon as they were seated, he asked, "Sondra, have you given away anything of Miller's?"

She gave him a surprised look. "Some of the furniture went to the Battered Women's Society." When he nodded and still looked as if he expected more, she continued, "His clothes and books went to the bunkhouse."

"Miller put his money into the ranch, not into things," Dylan said. "My wife was generous, though. She gave me that antique cavalry blanket—"

The sheriff whistled under his breath.

"—and Miller's favorite pocket knife. She made sure each of the hands got something special of Miller's, but why don't you tell us what this is all about?"

"What about Miller's rodeo buckles?"

"Oh." Sondra smiled. "Miller kept those in a case in the bottom drawer. They're beautiful. I thought maybe I'd have them framed."

"So you didn't give them away." The sheriff squinted at her.

"No. Why?"

"Those aren't just pretty, honey. They're valuable." Dylan and Troy exchanged a look.

"Anywhere from one hundred to five thousand dollars apiece." The sheriff bent down and put a box on his desk.

Sondra gaped at it. "That's Miller's!"

The sheriff opened the lid. "And the buckles?"

"Miller's," Dylan grated.

"I can confirm that by the event dates on some of them, but others are antiques and can't be traced. I needed you to confirm these were his and hadn't been given away."

"I've seen a file on the computer. I can e-mail it to you," Sondra said.

Tense as could be, Dylan demanded, "How did you get these?"

"The tire tracks we found by the fencing when the cattle were poisoned narrowed the make and model."

"So they were poisoned. It wasn't an accident." Sondra looked at Dylan.

He readjusted Matt in his arms. "I didn't have solid proof. Just a strong hunch."

"We've been following leads. When we searched the car, we found these and something else." The sheriff picked up a clear plastic envelope and laid it on the desk.

Sondra leaned forward and froze. The bag contained a pair of wedding bands. One was cut. *Kenny's and mine.*

❧

"Can you identify these?" Troy asked as Dylan watched his wife's reaction.

She nodded. "They're my wedding set—my old one."

"Are you sure?" the sheriff pressed.

"Yes." She turned to Dylan. "Someone has been in our house."

"Miller's brother," Dylan confirmed.

"But I wrote and asked if there was something he'd like to have. He made it clear he didn't want anything." Her voice shook. "He didn't have to sneak in and steal."

"Troy?" Someone from the doorway waved an envelope. "It's a match."

"Book him and add arson to the charges." Troy looked at Dylan. "Matched his footprint."

Dylan grimaced. "Why?"

"He invested his inheritance in that developing company."

Tears filled Sondra's eyes. "I would have given him the buckles."

But she's upset about Kenny's ring. That galled Dylan. No matter how much he loved her, her heart still belonged to another man.

"Thanks for coming in." Troy rose.

Dylan took the hint. They'd come and identified the stolen goods. There wouldn't be any more sabotage. He and Sondra stood. The rings on her left hand sparkled as she reached for the diaper bag. To his surprise, she didn't look back at the rings on the desk. She reached for Matt and snuggled him close.

"We already logged in this evidence. You're welcome to take it home."

"That would be nice." To Dylan's surprise, Sondra didn't sound desperately relieved. She looked up at him. "Maybe someday Matt would like those rings."

The sheriff nodded. "That's a fine idea. Speaking of rings, no one reckoned you'd slip a ring on Sondra's finger and secure the Curly Q at the last minute. Edwin's sabotage almost worked."

Dylan shook his head. "My plan was to make the Curly Q turn a stellar profit so Sondra would know I wanted her for herself—not for her land. The sabotage moved up the date is all. The provision in the will was just an excuse for me to wed this woman. I'd have done so in the months ahead."

Troy chuckled. "I guessed as much. Folks have had a high old time watching you fall for Sondra."

"I fell all right." Dylan looked into Sondra's eyes. He was taking a huge leap of faith here, but he'd been about to speak with her back home. God opened a door for him to tell Sondra how he felt, and he couldn't slam it shut. "What started out as a simple partnership between us because of Miller's will grew into something soul-deep."

Tears glittered in her eyes. She dropped the diaper bag and slipped her hand into his.

He added, "What started out as accepting Miller's will turned into following God's will."

They headed toward home, but Sondra remained silent. Dylan couldn't take it anymore. "We've gotta talk."

Sondra leaned against the headrest and closed her eyes. "Last time we had a serious talk in the car, we agreed Matt would call you daddy."

"Things there are settled. It's the you-me stuff that needs ironing out. I just announced that I love you, and you haven't said a thing."

She hitched her shoulder and looked out the window. "You didn't exactly say you love me. I understand. You said this wasn't a Valentine's-y, romantic marriage. I know you do love me—as your Christian sister."

Dylan pulled over to the side of the road. In the end, it all boiled down to this. "Is that all I am to you? Just your brother in the Lord? Someone you married because you think this was God's will, even if it wasn't yours?"

Very slowly, she turned toward him. Her eyes opened and filled with tears. "No. You and Matt and Jesus—you're my whole world." Her voice broke. "But I understand that love can be one-sided. I haven't done anything to deserve your love."

"Honey pie, I'm wild about you. God taught us that love isn't earned. It's freely given. Believe me, I have a heart full of love to give you." He proved it, too, with a heated kiss. He pulled away and pressed his forehead to hers. "Believe me, I'm not feeling very brotherly right now. I'm crazy in love with you."

She tilted her head and kissed him, then slowly pulled away. "Mmm. Then stay crazy, because I love you."

Dylan hastily buckled her seat belt and started the car. He pulled out onto the road and sped toward home.

"Dylan, what are you doing?"

"Speeding. I'd pay a million dollar ticket without batting an eye."

"You would? Why?"

He gave her a long look, and his voice dropped to a rumble. "It's time to go home, city-girl."

❧

Half an hour later, Sondra sat on the edge of the bed and pleated the satin of her nightgown between nervous fingers. Dylan came into the bedroom, gave her a searching look, and said, "We have a problem."

Her hand curled, smashing the satin into a ball. "We do?"

He surveyed the pillows, then lifted his chin. "Yup, we do." He didn't bat an eye or pause to take a breath. "You're on my side of the bed."

"I'm. . . ."

"On my side of the bed. I'll try to be workable on lots of issues, but this is one time when I'm going to be stubborn."

"Oh." She hopped up, wound her arms around his waist, and laughed.

"Now this is the way things are supposed to be."

epilogue

Sondra's laughter shivered in the morning air. "Hey, Dylan!" She came out of the henhouse holding a squirming, twenty-inch reptile. Extending it toward him, she grinned playfully. "Proud of me? I'm not petrified this time."

Dylan felt everything inside of him lurch.

Completely oblivious to his reaction, she launched into a rendition of the speech he'd given her the last time she'd found a snake. "This is a common milk snake. They've been known to eat eggs. They certainly don't eat people. Stop spluttering, Dylan! I learned my lesson from you that first day. If anything, the poor thing is terrified of me. Can't say as I blame him, either. Talk about a bad hair day!"

Dylan made a strangled sound and reached for his sheath knife. "Sondra, heave that snake away!"

"Oh, stop getting crazy. I'm not afraid of him." She turned her hands so she and the snake were facing one another. Playfully, she stuck out her tongue a few times. "He's kind of cute, don't you think?"

"Now, Sondra—toss him!"

"I'm going to take him over closer to the fence so I can grab a hoe. You said I'm supposed to chop off his head, but the thought makes me a little sick to my stomach. Do you mind doing the honors?"

"Gladly! Just heave him as far away as you can."

"Boss—" Nickels's voice cut in. "I'll get him; you take care of her."

"You know," Sondra said as she twisted the snake to suit her will, "we talked about what to name the ranch. What do you think of—"

"Sondra!"

Sondra finally obeyed. She casually tossed the squirming reptile onto the ground just a few feet away. Dylan leapt and tackled her. They rolled over a few times and came to a stop with him lying fully on top of her.

"Wow, sweetheart," she whispered. "You really know how to knock a girl off her feet."

He forced a chuckle, then forked his fingers through her wild hair and kissed her until they were both breathless. "I'm never gonna get enough of you."

"You both okay, boss?"

"More than okay," Dylan said as he got to his feet and pulled Sondra upright. "Thanks for the coverage."

Nickels shook his head and pushed his hat back a bit. "Reckon you ought to teach that little city-gal wife of yours to be careful of copperheads."

"Oh, it wasn't a copperhead, Nickels—it was just a plain, old milk snake." Sondra's smile froze, then melted as she saw the look the men exchanged. She could feel the blood draining from her face. Unwilling to let them witness her embarrassing cowardice, she vaguely murmured, "We all have chores to do." Just a few more steps, and she could sit down on the bench Dylan put in her garden. . . .

"Whoa. Hey." Dylan caught her and chuckled. He got her to the bench and promptly tucked her head between her watery knees.

When she finally sat up again, he asked, "Better?"

"Yeah. Fine."

"Coulda fooled me. You know, the first time you saw a snake, you lost your breakfast. This time, you nigh unto fainted. Looks like I've saddled myself with a prissy little city-gal for a wife."

"Almost right." She rested her head on his shoulder. "I'm definitely your wife, but I'm not prissy, and it wasn't the snake."

"Oh? And what was it?"

"Morning sickness."

Dylan took a minute to digest that news. Once it sank in, he let out a loud whoop.

Nickels came running. "Boss?"

Dylan chortled and gave Sondra a big kiss. "Praise God! We're gonna have another baby!"

A Letter To Our Readers

Dear Reader:

In order that we might better contribute to your reading enjoyment, we would appreciate your taking a few minutes to respond to the following questions. We welcome your comments and read each form and letter we receive. When completed, please return to the following:

Fiction Editor
Heartsong Presents
PO Box 719
Uhrichsville, Ohio 44683

1. Did you enjoy reading *In His Will* by Cathy Marie Hake?
   ❑ Very much! I would like to see more books by this author!
   ❑ Moderately. I would have enjoyed it more if

   _____

   _____

   _____

2. Are you a member of **Heartsong Presents**? ❑ Yes ❑ No
   If no, where did you purchase this book? _____

   _____

3. How would you rate, on a scale from 1 (poor) to 5 (superior), the cover design? _____

4. On a scale from 1 (poor) to 10 (superior), please rate the following elements.

   ____ Heroine   ____ Plot
   ____ Hero   ____ Inspirational theme
   ____ Setting   ____ Secondary characters

5. These characters were special because? _____

_____

_____

6. How has this book inspired your life? _____

_____

_____

7. What settings would you like to see covered in future
   Heartsong Presents books? _____

_____

_____

8. What are some inspirational themes you would like to see
   treated in future books? _____

_____

_____

9. Would you be interested in reading other **Heartsong
   Presents** titles? ❑ Yes ❑ No

10. Please check your age range:
   ❑ Under 18   ❑ 18-24
   ❑ 25-34   ❑ 35-45
   ❑ 46-55   ❑ Over 55

Name_____

Occupation _____

Address _____

City, State, Zip_____

VIRGINIA *Hearts*

3 stories in 1

There modern Northern Virginians discover love is waiting in their own backyard. Joelle Jamison seeks dating advice from a childhood friend who's loved her all her life; Lexie Zoltan struggles with an old flame's ideas for the future; and Reece Parker's aunt hides a treasure map to romance within her will.

Contemporary, paperback, 368 pages, 5³/₁₆" x 8"

_____

Heartsong